The Callahan Cousins

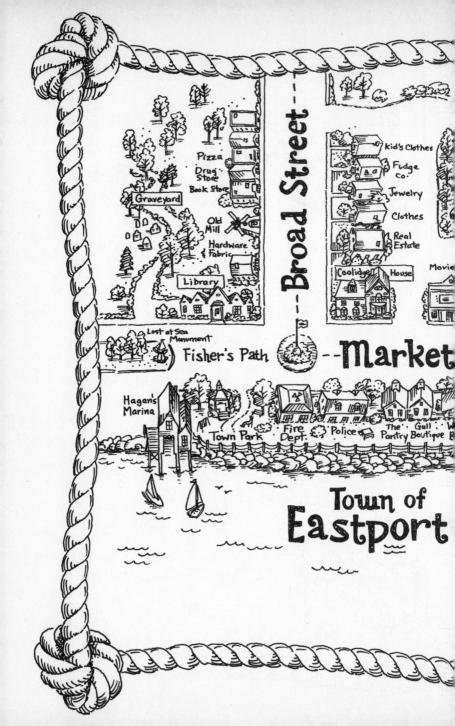

The Callahan Cousins

Keeping Cool

by Elizabeth Doyle Carey

LITTLE, BROWN AND COMPANY

New York · Boston · London

Little, Brown and Company

Time Warner Book Group
1271 Avenue of the Americas, New York, NY 10020
Visit our Web site at www.lb-teens.com

The characters and events portrayed in this book are fictitious.
Any similarity to real persons, living or dead, is coincidental
and not intended by the author.

First Edition: May 2006

Library of Congress Cataloging-in-Publication Data

Carey, Elizabeth Doyle.
Keeping cool / by Elizabeth Doyle Carey. — 1st ed.
p. cm. — (The Callahan cousins)
Summary: The twelve-year-old Callahan cousins are staying at their
grandmother's rambling seaside estate for a whole summer without parents, but
when the usually shy Kate tries to become the "cool" girl in town, her antics
threaten to pull the cousins apart.
ISBN-13: 978-0-316-73693-0 (hardcover)
ISBN-10: 0-316-73693-7 (hardcover)
[1. Cousins — Fiction. 2. Popularity — Fiction. 3. Islands — Fiction.
4. Grandmothers — Fiction.] I. Title.
PZ7.C2123Kee 2006
[Fic] — dc22   2005031107

10 9 8 7 6 5 4 3 2 1

Q-MT

Printed in the United States of America

Book design by Alyssa Morris

The text was set in Mrs. Eaves and the display was set in Bickley Script

For Alex, Liam, Finn, and new baby Niall: an ocean of love to you all. And a big welcome to the newest crop of cousins: Lily, Bea, Honey, and Arthur.
Cousins forever!

⌒

Special thanks to early enthusiasts and ongoing cheerleaders: Cat Osborne, Tiffany Palmer, Adriana Payne, Victoria Rotenstreich, Jennifer Sheehan, and Gretchen Werwaiss (ant connoisseur); and to Elaine George, Ayesha McFadden, and Juliet Imhof, without whom this book would not have been written.
Seriously.

"Send them to me," said grandma Gee.
And so they did.

CHAPTER ONE

Gee's Request

The interior of the muffin was golden yellow, with a fine crumb that was moist but not dense. Mini chocolate chips were nestled throughout, suspended like sweet stars in a baked galaxy. The chips were semisweet chocolate, and slightly melted to the point of softness, but not runny. The top of the muffin was butter glazed and sprinkled with granulated sugar, so it made a satisfying crunch when Kate bit into it again. She chewed and then sighed blissfully. But her pen was poised above the open page of her leather-bound recipe journal, and she didn't know what to write.

Kate called across her grandmother Gee's sunny yellow kitchen. "Sheila?"

"Yes, luv," Sheila's reply was distracted because she was mixing up another batch of muffins — blueberry ones this time — for a committee meeting that Gee was having at her house later that morning. Coffee, orange juice, and an assortment of minimuffins were on the menu, and Gee always joked that the various boards and committees she was on always wanted to have their meetings at her house, The Sound, so that they could stuff themselves with more of Sheila's fine cooking.

Kate was suffering from professional envy at the moment. She was really into cooking and baking, and she'd spent plenty of time at Sheila's side this summer, watching her technique, and dutifully recording in her journal the recipes that Sheila had committed to memory and then tweaked over the years. But despite the fact that Kate was known back home as an amazing cook, she could never seem to replicate the skill of her grandmother's longtime cook and housekeeper.

"Tell me one more time about the baking powder. Because every time I bake at sea level, everything comes out flat."

And Sheila was off and running again in her Irish accent, detailing oven temperature, ingredient ratios, mixer speeds, and any number of things that non-bakers would find excruciatingly boring, but that Kate found endlessly fascinating. Kate's pink pen struggled to keep up with the advice flowing from Sheila, and her tongue protruded from her mouth slightly as she concentrated on her penmanship. Her recipe journals were sacred — this one was her fifth — and since she intended to keep them forever (and possibly even publish them as a book one day, or use them to start a cooking school or television show), they had to be legible and pretty to look at.

Kate was sitting at the long wooden kitchen table in the corner of the kitchen, a large, many-paned window behind her looked out over the terrace, the pool, the rolling lawn, and then the wide blue expanse of the sound. It was a hot, bright day already, even though it was only seven fifteen, and the haze that enveloped Gull Island threatened only to gather strength as the day wore on, rather than dissipate. Kate sighed. She did not do well in the heat, even if she tried to dress for it.

Right now, Kate was wearing a sleeveless pink Lacoste shirt and a pair of white Bermuda shorts, with a pink and green ribbon belt. Her shoulder-length, chestnut brown hair was held back in a ponytail, and on her feet were Tretorn sneakers and low athletic socks with a tiny pink pom-pom at the heel. She wore a classic tank watch with a ribbon band she could change whenever she wanted (to match her outfits), and a thin gold chain around her neck. On her right hand she wore the gold Claddagh ring that Gee had given her and her three cousins earlier in the summer. It was a pair of hands holding a heart with a crown on it, and it was an Irish symbol of love and loyalty.

Much to her disappointment, she was not wearing earrings, since her ears — unlike her cousins' — were not pierced. Although she winced at the idea of the pain, and felt vaguely nauseated at the concept of holes through her ears, it was one form of suffering she was willing to endure, with the end goal so satisfying. Pierced ears were cool. Her parents had told her that she could have her ears pierced when she turned thirteen, but even though that birthday would soon be upon her, it wasn't soon enough. Her naked earlobes made her feel like a baby. And after all, they were *her* ears! as Kate often told her parents.

The screen door banged and in so doing announced the arrival of Kate's cousins Hillary, Neeve, and Phoebe, up from the Dorm — the little guesthouse at the bottom of Gee's property that they had recently redecorated and claimed as their own. Kate's heart sank when she heard the door, and it wasn't because she was unhappy to see the cousins. Rather, it meant that her cozy time in the kitchen with Sheila was soon to come to an end for another morning, and she'd be off to sailing clinic — a daily event that she dreaded for most of the twenty hours of each day that she wasn't there.

"Good morning, my little chickadees," Kate chirped, in her best imitation of Gee.

Phoebe grunted, and Kate tsk-tsked her. "Bee, you'll never be a morning person if you keep staying up until all hours to read your book." She loved to torture Phoebe in the morning. Next she turned to Hillary. "Hilly-billy, don't forget your sunscreen today. You made me promise to remind you, so there. I did. And Neeve . . ."

"Oh, buzz off, old lady," said Neeve with a mischievous twinkle in her eye that let Kate know she was only teasing. "I've gotten by pretty well this far in my life without your busy-bee routine." Neeve poured herself a mug of black coffee and sat down at the kitchen table. She picked off the corner of a muffin from the platter, and nibbled it without even noticing the fine qualities that had sent Kate into cascades of rapture only moments earlier. Phoebe, meanwhile, rested her head in her hands and read the front page of the *Boston Globe,* her white-blond hair hanging in front of her face like a curtain drawn for privacy. And Hillary went to pour herself a bowl of granola.

"Fine." Kate smiled but she folded her arms across her chest in mock-anger at Neeve. "Fine, then. I won't remind you to bring Band-Aids for your blisters. You're on your own. You can just . . ."

Neeve stood up and placed her palms on the table; then she leaned as far across the table as her tiny frame allowed, until she was only inches from Kate's face. "You. Just. Did." She sat back down and shook her head slowly from side to side in a pantomime of amazement. Her black cowlicks jumped and shone in the light from the iron chandelier that hung overhead.

"Pee-yew!" Kate waved her hand frantically in front of her face, and scrunched up her nose in disgust. "Somebody forgot to brush her teeth this morning!" she teased, getting Neeve back.

Hillary was smiling at the exchange as she came to the table with her bowl. Her strawberry blond curls were wet and pulled back into a hasty ponytail, and her freckled skin was fresh and scrubbed-looking. Her Goretex shorts and fitted Lycra tank, combined with her running shoes and her rangy, muscular limbs, offered little doubt as to who was the athlete of the group. "Oh! Kate? Could you help me with this photo collage I'm making? I want to send it to Lucy back home, and it just looks so lame right now."

"Sure." Kate had a great eye, and was always sprucing things up for the others, or helping them with projects.

"Hey, what's for snack today?" Neeve asked Kate.

"Snickerdoodles," Kate replied.

"Yes!" said Neeve and Hillary simultaneously; they high-fived, and Kate shook her head at them.

"Savages," she laughed. "All you think about is food."

"We're growing girls!" said Hillary.

"Here ya's go, grow on this!" Sheila hustled over to the table with a plate of perfectly flat, perfectly crisp bacon that she'd cooked in the oven at 450 degrees, and Hillary and Neeve fell upon it greedily. Kate reopened her journal, though, and asked, "Do you pre-heat the pan first and then put the bacon on it?"

Sheila sighed in amused exasperation. "Some days I do, luv, and some days I don't. It depends on where me head is at in the mornin'!" But she tousled Kate's hair affectionately, and swiped at her with a dishrag to show her she didn't really mind all the questions.

Kate made a note of this on her bacon page. Then she put down her journal and pulled her To Do book out of her tote bag that lay on the floor next to her chair. This was a spiral-bound, pocket-sized book — disposable by nature, since she'd tear out the sheets as she completed the tasks listed on each side of a page.

"Oh dear," she said aloud. "I've got to buy three birthday cards and send them out today to Julia, Caroline, and Holly back home. And I've got to get going on that needlepoint eyeglasses case for *Gee's* birthday. I need more needlepoint thread for that," she was muttering now as she thought out loud. Kate never missed a birthday — she loved celebrating with other people and could always be counted on for a cake and a nice present. Her friends back home adored her for it, since she'd always make a fuss over them, and every March, when her birthday rolled around, people went crazy trying to dream up inventive presents and treats for *her,* for a change. "Oh, also, we need soap for the Dorm, and *toothpaste*" — Kate shot a fakestern look at Neeve — "hmm. What else?"

"Good morning, my little chickadees!" trilled Gee as she came in the back door. Her short snow-white hair was flat but dry after her usual morning swim in the sound, thanks to her trusty bathing cap. Neeve and Hillary exchanged a private smirk at Gee's greeting, which had been so effortlessly replicated by Kate only moments earlier.

"Hi, Gee!" they called back in greeting.

"I'm just going to run up for a quick shower, and then I've got something important to discuss with all of you before you dash off to clinic. Be right back!" And with a flutter of her fingers and a swish of her white terrycloth robe, she was up the stairs, like a white butterfly borne aloft on the breeze.

The girls looked at each other questioningly. Even Phoebe lifted her head. Across the room, there was a *chunk* as Sheila slid the rye bread down into the toaster for Gee's customary breakfast.

Hillary shrugged first. "Beats me," she said. And then, "Phoebe, could I please see the Sports section?"

Phoebe handed it over and then went back to her paper, and Neeve and Kate were left looking at each other.

"Do you think we've done something wrong?" Kate asked in a whisper. She was wracking her brain to think of what it could've been. She'd basically never been in trouble in her life, but now that she was hanging out with the cousins, anything could happen — even getting in trouble.

"Nah," Neeve waved away the very idea of it (not that she would have been nervous even if they were in trouble; Neeve was used to breaking rules on a regular basis). "She never waits to tell us when we've done something wrong. Plus, we usually know it when we have." She grinned and wiggled her eyebrows up and down. "Anyway, it's not like there's much that anyone could do wrong with Gee. Especially you!" She shook her head and held her hand out to Phoebe without even looking at her. "International news, please."

"Not done yet," was Phoebe's terse reply.

"Arts section, please," said Neeve, without missing a beat.

And boom, it was in her hand.

That left Kate. "Cooking section?" she asked hopefully.

"Wednesdays."

"Oh." Kate looked around at her cousins, and felt a rush of fondness and admiration for each of them. They were so different from one another — although the family resemblance was strong enough for strangers to remark on it (particularly the ice-blue Callahan eyes that they'd all inherited from Gee by way of their fathers) — but each girl brought something to this summer stay at Gee's house that had made their time here together very enriching and enlightening for Kate, although not always in a good way.

Neeve was the most unique of the group. She and her younger brother and sister had lived all over the world (Ireland, Kenya, China, and now Singapore) because her dad was in the U.S. Foreign Service and her mom was from Ireland. She had friends in wild places, and lots of unusual makeup, and she could speak some exotic languages. Plus she was a really good dresser; she made up zany outfits out of odds and ends that always managed to look effortlessly cool on her tiny pixieish figure, and she wore scads of jewelry — bracelets, and tribal necklaces, and really cool pierced earrings all the time. And although her short black hair sprung up in cowlicks all over her head, her confidence and her little heart-shaped face so full of fun and mischief would make any observer wish that she had black hair and cowlicks sticking up everywhere, too.

Kate looked at Hillary. Hillary wasn't super-stylish like Neeve, but she was very brave; nothing scared her or grossed her out. As an only child, Hillary didn't mind doing things on her own (unlike Kate, who *hated* being alone), and she never needed a buddy to hold her hand or boost her confidence. She was really athletic and strong, long and lean with muscles you could actually see. She was into stuff like science and the environment, and she was forever camping out in Colorado where she was from, or shooting down some whitewater rapids with her dad. Hillary dressed really casually for the most part, in her Sweetie Sweats and other kinds of training gear, and her strawberry blond curls always seemed to be wet from an after-workout shower or from swimming, but she had a real image: tomboy, adventurer, cowgirl.

And then there was Phoebe. She was from Florida, and she was really, really, really super-smart and well-read, with an amazing vocabulary. She knew a lot about everything and was very mature. And even though she wasn't brave like Hillary, she could sometimes make Kate feel like a wimp by being so haughty and grown-up acting all the time. She was never emotional like Kate, and she was never babyish — she was just poised, contained, and sure of herself. Also, Phoebe was beautiful: tall and willowy, with white-blond hair that she'd inherited from her gorgeous Swedish mother, the bright blue Callahan eyes, and dark golden skin. But the annoying thing was that she didn't care about her looks at all! In fact, she actually kind of hid them, dressing like a hippie (albeit a neat one), and wearing reading glasses and ugly buns in her hair and stuff. A classic bookworm.

Kate herself was neither tall nor thin, just regular (or, okay, a little chubby). She was very cute, with a tiny upturned nose and a spray of freckles, creamy skin, and bright blue eyes. Both preppy and girly, Kate favored the color pink, and the only strong physical feats she was known for were her hugs, which were legendary and generously doled out. Her mouth turned up at the corners in a natural smile, and her bubbly laugh was contagious and frequent. She wasn't internationally intriguing, or western rugged, or a brainiac; she was a daydreamer and a cozy homebody who liked to spoil people, creating beautiful or delicious things that pleased people's senses (food, needlepoint, hand-knit sweaters, watercolors, flower arrangements, harmonious room décor). Kate was beloved by her friends (which were legion), and always had a positive effect on people — you couldn't help but smile at her. Back home, everyone liked to gather at Kate's, and when they weren't there, her friends called her house constantly for her advice on everything from fights with friends to room decor. Kate's parents and teachers were always praising her sensitivity, saying it was a gift, and that she was compassionate beyond her years.

But this summer, Kate's sensitivity — both physical and emotional — had been feeling more like a curse, as the cousins plunged into one stressful project after another. Already this summer, they'd searched for and found a lost island and settled an old family rivalry against Sloan Bicket, the girls' sometime friend and sometime enemy; they'd unearthed a family secret about Neeve's dad that had been unpleasant; and they'd redecorated the Dorm, which had caused some serious rivalry and infighting between Kate and Neeve. Kate had never felt like such a chicken until she'd been thrown into this series of nerve-racking situations that consistently highlighted her shortcomings, rather than her strengths. Of course, in the end, all of their projects always turned out all right, but along the way, Kate was stressed, and scared, and lately, embarrassed to realize that she'd taken on the role of the group's whiny crybaby.

Also, somewhere along the way this summer, she'd become the group's scapegoat. The others liked to tease her, and she had egged them on in the beginning, loving the attention. She'd played up her fears and her reluctance to participate in things because it made the others laugh and focus on her; but now the cousins — Phoebe in particular — teased her mercilessly all the time. Kate was tired of it, and it wasn't funny anymore. She had started to feel like a total loser, which was not how she felt back home.

Kate snapped out of her daze and glanced at her watch. Oh dear. Ten minutes until they had to get on their bikes and ride to clinic. Kate hated bike riding; it was so tiring and here on Gull she was always the slowest. Back home, she and her friends took leisurely bike rides for pleasure — they didn't race out the door and get on their bikes first thing, already late and rushing to be on time. But Gee couldn't very well load four bikes into the back of her Volvo wagon every morning to take them to Hagan's Marina, and somehow, getting themselves — all four of them — out the door each morning was hectic *and* slow.

Kate stood up to prepare the snack for clinic. She'd started doing this about two weeks ago — first just packing something for herself, then for the cousins, too. Now, so many of the other kids, and counselors, even, stopped by to see what she'd brought, that she'd had to start baking something special the night before just to be sure she had enough.

Snickerdoodle cookies were Kate's specialty. She crossed the kitchen to the butcher block island where she'd left the cookies cooling on racks the night before. Now, she prepared a Tupperware container by lining it with waxed paper, and then neatly arranging the cookies in rows and then layers, separating each layer with a sheet of waxed paper. She finished and pressed the lid down tightly, and went to put the box in her tote bag. She couldn't turn the box on its side or all of the cookies would get jostled and break, so she carefully removed the items from her bag, stowed the container on the bottom of the bag, and then replaced the neatly folded extra clothes and bathing suit, the little cosmetics bag filled with sunscreen, Band-Aids, bug repellent, zinc oxide, calamine lotion, Handi-Wipes, and alcohol swabs, her To Do book and pen, a map of the island, Ziploc bags for wet bathing suits (the other cousins never remembered to bring them, no matter how often Kate reminded them!) her long-billed baseball cap (great sun protection), and a small flashlight and whistle that she carried everywhere with her, just in case. True, the bag was heavy, but Kate liked to be organized and prepared for any eventuality or mishap. And although she hated lugging the bag, she felt it was her duty to the group — her contribution to their well-being.

There. That was done. She stood up and brushed her hands together, whisking off imaginary bits of dust or dirt. And right then, Gee returned, showered and immaculately dressed, right down to her peach-and-white Jack Rogers sandals and her coordinating coral-colored pedicure. Gee was beautiful in an outdoorsy way, with tanned skin, the ice-blue eyes, and the tousled white hair (very much like Neeve's, save for the color). Because she swam in the sound every day, she was slim and toned and radiated an energy and enthusiasm for life that belied her age. Her perfect nails and matching lipstick, coupled with her understated but elegant way of dressing (crisp white tailored pants, a fine gold belt, a neat blue-and-white-striped short-sleeved silk sweater that tucked perfectly into her pants) showed that she took care to look nice, but wasn't obsessed by it.

Kate looked at her expectantly, eager to be reassured that they'd done nothing wrong (although as Neeve had just pointed out, Gee had very few rules about things. All she wanted was for them to be kind, enthusiastic, safe, and well-mannered). Gee poured herself a cup of coffee, grabbed her plate of buttered toast from the counter, shot a grateful smile at Sheila, and came to sit at the head of the table, in her customary seat. She placed her mug on the table and then laid her hands, palms down, on either side of her green Toile place mat.

"Girls, I need your help."

Four pairs of identical blue eyes met Gee's, the same color as their own. Kate pulled out her chair and sat back down, surprised by the excitement in Gee's voice.

Gee continued. "As you know, every summer we hold a big dinner dance here at The Sound, a benefit, with all proceeds going to the medical clinic that my father founded here on Gull Island." The girls nodded and Gee continued. "One of the things we do is hold an auction and a raffle, which both offer wonderful items donated from businesses around the island."

"Yes! One time my dad won a bike in the raffle," said Kate, smiling at the memory of her dad's description of his joy at winning.

"Oh! That's supposed to be such a fun party!" squealed Neeve, ever the social butterfly. "That's the one where you get a tent in the yard, and tons of people come, and there's a band, and caterers?"

"Exactly," agreed Gee with a smile and a nod of her head. "Now unfortunately, the woman who usually organizes the items for the auction and raffle had her back go out on her this year, poor thing, and we're quite behind in soliciting donations for the two venues. I wondered if you might be willing to go around the island and talk to people about donating." Gee looked at them hopefully and leaned in to take a quick bite of her toast while she awaited their replies.

"Totally!" Neeve nearly choked on her black coffee, she was so excited. She loved meeting new people and mingling and chatting. Hillary and Phoebe — one brave and one game for adventures — both murmured their assent, but Kate did not like the idea at all. In fact, she thought Gee's request sounded scary. Just go up to strangers and ask them to give you stuff? No way! She got a pit in her stomach just thinking about it.

Sensing Kate's hesitation, Gee cocked her head to one side. "What do you think, Katie? Would you help?"

Now Kate's manners got the better of her; because after having Kate to her house for the whole summer without any parents, that Gee should think Kate wouldn't do this one thing to help her out was appalling. So Kate smiled brightly and summoned up an enthusiastic reply to mask her dread. "I'd love to do it! I'm already thinking of places and people we could ask," she fibbed.

"Thanks, dear. Thanks all of you." Gee was clearly relieved as she looked around the kitchen table. "We've only got a few weeks left, so the sooner you could get going on it, the better. I know some other people on the benefit committee were going to ask their children to help, too, so there should be quite a few of you out there. There might be some overlap, so don't be distressed if you go to a store and they've already been asked."

Neeve was already ticking off ideas on her fingers. "We should ask at The Dip, for, like, free Awful, Awful sundaes;

and we could ask Booker's, maybe for sailing gear or a tennis racquet, and at the Little Store, and maybe Talbot's dad would donate a fishing expedition on his boat. . . ."

Oh dear. Now Kate had to go out and talk to strangers, when all she really liked to do was stay home and bake, or paint, or work on one of her needlework projects. She rested her cheek on her hand and tried to distract herself by daydreaming about the dinner dance. What would the flower arrangements look like? Maybe the food would be delicious. . . .

But then, "Let's go, Katie!" commanded Neeve, bossy as ever. The others were already standing at the back door, tote bags full of sailing gear slung over their shoulders.

Kate sighed and stood up. Gee had gone to answer the phone, which rang off the hook all day wherever Gee was, and Sheila was now whipping up some kind of pie crust for dinner. The kitchen was fragrant and productive, and Kate wished she could stay. She grabbed her bag and one last muffin for the ride, then followed the others out to the garage to claim a red bike. Over the years, Gee's nine children had had so many bikes lost or stolen that Gee had finally asked Mr. Addison, the gardener, to spray-paint all of the remaining bikes entirely red (wheels, spokes, handlebars — *everything!*) so that they'd always be recognizable as Callahan bikes by everyone on Gull. Her thought was that no one would be able to steal them then, but the kids all pointed out that the system only worked because no one *wanted* to steal all-red bikes. *No wonder my dad was so happy to win a new bike,* thought Kate, smiling in spite of the knot in her stomach.

The other three were chattering happily about the raffle and the auction, bantering as they tossed ideas back and forth. Kate decided to pretend it wasn't going to happen; that was the only way to deal with it for now. Instead, she dreamily inhaled the scent of blooming honeysuckle in the still, already hot air. She stowed her tote bag in the basket of her bike, and paused to pick a particularly gorgeous pink rose from the climbing vine that currently threatened to smother the garage. Gee had told her that it was called "Old Blush," and that it had been blooming in America for hundreds of years — her gardening reference book called it a "tough, dependable pioneer." But Kate loved it because it smelled great, and the soft petals were such a perfect shade of her favorite color. Pink roses were her trademark — girly and sweet, but hardier than she realized.

CHAPTER TWO

The New Me

*A*ll the way to clinic, Kate was dead-last in the line of four biking cousins, as usual. She liked to tell herself that it was so she could keep an eye on the others, in case one of them got hurt, but the truth was, she wasn't fast and daring like the others, and she did like to enjoy the scenery as she rode, trying to make the ride somewhat pleasant each day by spotting a new flower or pretty bird along the way.

The open causeway that connected the summer resort area of Gull Island (known as North Wing) with the busier town end (South Wing) was devoid of cars. The sound stretched out to her right — flat and glassy in the heat — and a few optimistic sailboats sat with limp sails on the horizon, hoping for a puff of air. The day was decidedly hot now, and the hair underneath her ponytail was wet. Kate was out of breath and her leg muscles burned, and maybe it was just from the effort of biking, but her skin already sizzled from the sun. She wished she could get tan, instead of just turning red all the time. Tan people never seemed miserable when they were outdoors.

Kate coasted for a minute, and sat up straight to wipe her arm across her perspiring upper lip. The cousins' new semi-friend Lark Kendo was up ahead, turning into the Hagan's Marina parking lot, and Kate watched as the others met up with her and began chatting animatedly, about the clinic benefit, no doubt. She wondered if Lark was participating in the donations-getting, but she was too far back to catch up and ask.

A few minutes later, Kate entered the Hagans' headquarters: a small, wooden A-frame house that served as the base for their sailing school and various other nautical programs and businesses the Hagans ran. Kids were milling around, waiting for clinic to start, and the counselors — teenagers and college-age kids — were standing in a group around the soda machine, laughing about a party one of them had hosted the night before.

Kate caught sight of Sloan Bicket dead ahead, and her stomach dropped. She couldn't face the potentially evil Sloan this early on a Monday morning without the others. She looked to see where the cousins were and began to veer away from Sloan. But at the last minute, Sloan spotted her and called out, "Hey, Callahan!"

Kate gulped and looked over her shoulder. Surely Sloan was calling to Neeve or Hillary. But no, they were out on the dock already, getting their life preservers on. Oh dear. She turned back to Sloan and flashed a questioning look at her, like *"Who, me?"*

"Yeah, c'mere!" Sloan ordered, and her long, thin fingers flicked impatiently as she waved Kate over.

Half-flattered and half-scared, Kate slowly moved toward her, as if in a dream. Sloan was cool and commanding, and Kate was pleased to have been singled out, but she wasn't sure what she was being singled out for.

"Hi," Kate croaked nervously when she joined Sloan. Her mouth had dried out on her arduous journey across the room, but she still had the presence of mind to notice the tiny gold seashells nestled in Sloan's pierced earlobes and wonder how much it had hurt when she got them.

Sloan was all business as she swung her long, glossy, pin-straight brown hair over one deeply tanned shoulder. "I just want to make it perfectly clear to you Callahans that I don't want you going to any of the places where I have connections."

"What?" Kate laughed nervously. Her anxiety at talking to Sloan distracted her from understanding.

"For the benefit? Soliciting donations?" Sloan repeated, enunciating carefully, as if Kate were a dunce. Sloan tapped her foot and sighed impatiently.

"Oh." Relief flooded over Kate. Phew. Thank goodness it wasn't something they'd already done; it was something they could prevent. "Okay. Sure, Sloan. No problem. Whatever you say." Kate was happy to be able to comply with Sloan's wishes.

"'Cause if you do . . . there's going to be problems." Sloan spun on her heel and strode away, her darkly tanned legs endless in their short shorts.

"But wait . . ." Sloan didn't turn back. How were the Callahans supposed to know *where* Sloan had connections? Oh dear. Kate should've asked Sloan for a list. Now they'd be hitting spots in town without knowing that they should have avoided them. And then there'd be . . . *problems*. That sounded ominous, if just the tiniest bit vague. Nervously, Kate bit on her thumbnail, a habit left over from when she stopped sucking her thumb (not that long ago, truth be told). She only wanted to obey Sloan and avoid any kind of conflict, but how?

Confident Neeve would know what to do. Or Phoebe, super-smart as she was.

But Kate didn't get a chance to tell the cousins what had happened because by the time she'd found and put on a life preserver (clipped and pulled snugly around her), their instructor, Tucker, had already begun the day's lesson. It would have to wait.

"Totally outrageous!" Neeve declared for the fourteenth time, smacking the ice cream parlor's counter for emphasis. They had stopped by The Dip after clinic, needing sugar and air conditioning in order to discuss Sloan's evilness.

"She is just *so* rude!" agreed Hillary, shaking her head in amazement.

Kate's cousins had had the exact reaction she'd expected when she told them about her interaction with Sloan. She smiled.

"And obviously you told her we'd do no such thing?" Phoebe had said when Kate first told them of Sloan's order. Phoebe'd been swinging her legs from the spinning stool, and they'd stopped moving while Kate talked.

Kate's smiled faded. "Well, not exactly. I mean, we don't want to upset her, or, like, have her mad at us. And she said there'd be 'problems.' You know, that sounds serious." It had occurred to Kate during clinic that Sloan's threat might be her ticket out of the donation-solicitation business. Maybe if the others agreed that they should just stay out of it and leave it to Sloan, then they wouldn't have to do any of the dreaded asking? But even as she thought it, Kate knew the others wouldn't agree. None of them would do anything just to placate Sloan. In fact, it was more likely they'd do things specifically to make her mad. Kate shuddered just thinking about a mad Sloan.

Phoebe loathed Sloan even more than the rest of them did (Hillary was too clueless about girly-girl politics to even get half of what Sloan did, and Neeve was always so eager to socialize with new people that she would overlook a lot of bad behavior on Sloan's part). Now Phoebe continued her rant. "Imagine the nerve of that girl, telling us where we can and can't go on this island. This is a free country! Just because she's a year-rounder, she thinks she's cool, or something."

"Well, she is cool," Kate interjected quietly.

"Absolutely not. Nonsense!" Phoebe's nostrils flared, and she angrily redid her long, white-blond hair into a bun. "She's *far* from cool. She just *thinks* she is. And how dare she pick on you! I'm going to have it out with her this time, I'm telling you. I mean it!"

A deep blush washed over Kate's face as Phoebe spoke. "I can stick up for myself, Phoebe," she said quietly. She'd be mortified to have Phoebe fight her battles. Not that she was likely to fight them herself, but still . . .

But Phoebe and the others laughed. "You?! You couldn't stick up for a flea!" said Phoebe.

Kate's heart sank. It was true. She wasn't a fighter. Her shame must've been plain as day on her face, because Hillary scooted off her stool and came to wrap an arm around Kate's shoulder. Kate was the comforter in the group, so the other three were always at a bit of a loss when she was upset.

"Don't worry, Katie," said Hillary. "We'll find that Sloan and . . ."

"Beat the pants off her for you!" interjected Neeve.

Kate tried to summon a smile. "You don't need to fight my battles for me. I can manage perfectly well on my own."

Phoebe smiled indulgently at Kate and shook her head. "Come on, Katie," she teased. "You wouldn't even leave the house if it wasn't for us!"

Kate looked down at her hands. It was true, but she hated to admit it, so she didn't respond.

"Yeah, do you think you'd ever do anything fun or exciting on your own?" Neeve could be just as relentless as Phoebe in her teasing of Kate.

Kate considered this for about one second, then she squared her shoulders and looked up at them. "Of course! I'd go to the Old Mill and get supplies all on my own. I do it all the time!" The crafts store in town was her favorite thing about Gull Island. It was located in an old windmill and had shelves reaching all the way up to the top of its three-story height, each one laden with art or craft supplies.

Phoebe burst out laughing. "What's fun or exciting about going there? That place is for old ladies!"

Hillary and Phoebe giggled. "That's why Kate fits right in!" laughed Neeve.

Kate felt stung by this last comment. "Why are you guys going after me like this?" Back home, her friends all looked up to her; no one would ever rag on her like this.

Hillary squeezed her tightly and then went back to her stool. "Oh, we're not going after you. We're teasing you. It's just so fun! You're such an easy target!"

Kate took a deep breath and sat up very straight. "I am not an old lady."

Hillary patted her knee soothingly and said, "Of course not. We know that."

But Neeve said, "Then why are you always buying bunion cream and getting newsletters from the American Association of Retired People?!" And the others collapsed into laughter again.

"Fine," said Kate. "Just fine. But just you wait. I'm going to change, and you'll all be surprised."

"Okay, Katie!" said Phoebe sarcastically.

"Whatever you say, Old Lady Callahan!" said Neeve, and she and Phoebe laughed and slapped five.

Kate heaved a huge sigh and turned back to her Awful, Awful ice cream sundae ("They're Awful big, and Awful good!" The Dip proclaimed). She'd show them. Old lady. Harumph!

THE NEW ME
Makeover (get tan!)
Be braver
Get in shape
New interests
Pierce ears
Wear bikini

Kate put down her pink pen, laid her To Do book aside, and gazed out over the sound. She could hear the others up in the pool, shrieking as they sprayed each other with some silly new waterguns Gee had picked up for them. Needing a break from the cousins after town, Kate was sitting on a shady bench down in the bathing pavilion wearing a pink bikini that had sat in her drawer all summer since she'd felt too shy to wear it. (Okay, she was only wearing the bandeau-style top, with a pair of high-waisted shorts, but you had to start somewhere.) She was working on a list that had been germinating in her mind for some time, but had only just crystallized that afternoon.

Kate was dismayed by the exchange she'd had with Sloan that morning, and then especially by the other girls' reaction to it. Particularly, she was bothered by their calling her an old lady. And that was mostly because she knew it was true. She was tired of being teased by the others and she was tired of her image here on Gull; it was time for a change. And anyway, anything new that she learned here would go over well back home. Because back in Westchester, *she* was the leader — her friends looked up to *her*. Granted, they weren't a group that ran around acting like pirates and planting flags on islands, or digging up old family secrets like CIA agents, but they were fun and cool, too.

So she had thought about her cousins and *their* images, and how they could help her reinvent herself a little; and then she'd made a list that encompassed the ways she wanted to change, matching them up with the skills her cousins had to offer.

Kate stood up. She was excited by the prospect of reinventing herself; it was like a redecorating project, and she loved those! She walked quickly up from the bathing pavilion, eager to get the others involved.

"Freeze!" called Hillary as she neared the pool.

Neeve raised her water gun and took aim at Kate. "Put your hands up where I can see them or I'll shoot!" she ordered with an evil grin.

Kate was about to scream and run away, back down the hill. But then she thought of her new image (*Be braver!*), and instead put her hands in the air like claws and stomped toward the pool, hunching her back and pretending to be a ferocious monster.

Hillary and Neeve exchanged glances, and lowered their guns.

"Katie? Are you alright?" asked Neeve with real concern.

Kate dropped her hands to her side and stood up straight. She smiled. "Yeah, why?"

"Why didn't you run away screaming?"

"Um, because I thought it would be fun to play along for a change."

"Weird," said Neeve.

"Yeah," agreed Hillary. Hillary put her gun on the side of the pool and climbed out. She wrapped herself in a towel. Neeve followed suit, and then Phoebe.

"Hey! I was thinking about coming in!" Kate was actually kind of sad that they were all getting out.

"It's way too cold for you in there," said Neeve. "Anyway, I'm starving."

Phoebe agreed. "Me, too. Katie! What are we having for a snack this afternoon?"

Kate's eyes lit up. "Oh! I was thinking of . . ." But then she stopped abruptly. "I don't know," she said, in her plainest voice. "Why don't you go put something together for us?"

Again, Hillary and Neeve exchanged glances, but this time with Phoebe, too.

Phoebe's white eyebrows knit together in concern. "Katie, are you okay?"

Kate shrugged. She was trying to reinvent herself, do something unexpected, that's all. "Yes. I'm fine. Why?"

"Well, you played along with us, and then you wanted to come in the pool, and now you're bagging snack. You're just not yourself," said Hillary rationally.

Kate sat down primly on the end of one of the pink-and-white-flowered lounge cushions. She folded her hands and crossed one knee over the other. "That's what I'm here to talk to you about."

They looked at her. "Okay," said Neeve, scrubbing her wet hair with the end of the towel.

Kate took a deep breath. "I want to reinvent myself. And I need your help."

The others burst out laughing.

"Okay-y-y . . ." said Hillary, grinning. "So how can we help you?"

"Wait!" interrupted Phoebe. "Let me grab a snack first." She dashed into the kitchen and returned with a box of dry crackers, which she plunked on the table unceremoniously.

Hillary and Neeve looked at it in dismay. "*This* is a snack?" said Hillary, her voice heavy with disappointment.

"Kate always has little napkins, and something she's made

from scratch. And there are, like, lemon wedges floating in a pitcher of something." Neeve picked up the box of crackers while she spoke, examined it, and dropped it back down on the table where it landed with a rattle.

"Fine," said Phoebe, reaching for a cracker and taking a bite. "Then go get something yourselves, or convince Kate to make it." The cracker was super-dry and Phoebe herself winced as she tried to swallow it.

Kate nearly stood up to go make something, but she thought twice and stayed put. It was time for *them* to take care of *her* for a minute. The snack could wait. In fact, she wasn't even going to make snack for clinic tomorrow; she'd just decided. Let people fend for themselves for a change!

"So, I was thinking . . . ," she began. All eyes were upon her. "You know, you each kind of have a specialty. Like, Neeve is really stylish and cool, and Hillary's brave and athletic, and Phoebe is really smart and educated. . . . And I was thinking maybe each of you could, kind of, help me make myself over. Like a new and improved Kate. Better. Cooler . . ." She looked at them hopefully and folded her hands in her lap.

The others were silent for a moment while they considered her request. Neeve bit her cuticle thoughtfully, and Phoebe twisted her wet hair into a bun while she stared off at a fishing boat in the sound that was chugging back to port. Hillary sat down on a nearby lounge chair, flexing her calf muscles and then absentmindedly massaging them.

Kate looked at them expectantly. And waited. And waited.

She suddenly realized she'd been hoping for them to protest. To say she was great just like she was, and why would she ever want to change?

"Guys?" she prodded anxiously. They all snapped out of it and came back to life.

"Okay," said Neeve.

"Yeah, we could *try*," said Hillary.

"But you'd have to really be game," added Phoebe.

Kate gulped. "Uh . . . okay!" She forced a smile onto her face. "I *am* game. Really."

"We'll see about that!" said Neeve, with a grin. "We'll just see."

CHAPTER THREE

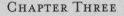

Cool

Sheila served dinner on the terrace that night. There was grilled halibut crusted with crushed almonds and served with a very light mustard cream sauce. The fish was accompanied by crisp *haricots verts* and a medley of roasted potatoes, and dinner was to be followed by a raspberry pie a la mode. Kate nearly had to tie herself to her chair to keep from running for her recipe journal, but she had decided to put her cooking ambitions on hold for the time being while she focused on her new self. Anyway, dinner turned out to be a brainstorming session about the donation-getting process, and Kate's terror kept her rooted to her seat, listening.

Gee ducked away right at the start of dinner to grab last year's auction and raffle catalog and fill them in on items they'd received as donations in the past. She lifted her tortoiseshell reading glasses on the chain around her neck, placed them on the tip of her tiny button nose, and began reading aloud as she quickly scanned the hundred or so items.

"Let's see. Dinner for four at Cabot's Clam Shack. A camping kit from Booker's, including tent, Coleman stove, lanterns, sleeping bags, and a walkie-talkie set. A two-cart supermarket spree at the Bicket Bouquet . . ."

The girls interrupted Gee with *"Boos."* Sloan's family owned the island grocery store, and Gee knew that the girls' rivalry with Sloan was just as strong as their fathers' rivalry with Sloan's father. But as she smiled in acknowledgment, she also put a finger to her lips to silence them; Sheila was Sloan's aunt (or half-aunt, since Sloan's dad was Sheila's much-younger half-brother). And although Sheila and Sloan made no secret of their dislike for one another, Gee felt it was bad manners for the Callahans to criticize Sloan when Sheila might overhear.

Phoebe got a wicked look on her face. "Maybe *we* should go solicit at the Bicket Bucket!" (She always intentionally mispronounced the name — within earshot of Sloan whenever possible.)

Kate was aghast. "No! Because of what Sloan said this morning?!" But then she clapped her hand over her mouth in regret. Oh, why had she said anything?! Now Gee would want to know all about the exchange with Sloan, and she'd get upset, and feel bad that she'd started this whole thing up. . . .

Kate slid her eyes around the table and saw the cousins' frantic looks. Neeve was drawing a finger across her own neck as if to say, "Stop. Shut up!" and Phoebe and Hillary were looking worriedly at Gee. Finally, Kate slid her eyes over to Gee, who was now leaning toward her, taking her glasses off, and peering intently at Kate over her empty plate.

"And what did Sloan say this morning?" asked Gee. From the tone of her voice, Kate could tell that Gee already knew something bad had happened. Nothing was ever good where Sloan was concerned.

Kate peeled her hand from her mouth and smiled her cheeriest smile. "Nothing!" she chirped. And she picked up her fork and chased the last green bean around her plate, pointedly not looking at Gee. But she could still feel Gee's eyes upon her. She glanced back at Gee guiltily.

"Okay, come clean, girls! What happened?" pressed Gee. She looked from face to face, but they'd rearranged their features into inscrutable masks of innocence.

"Nothing. Really," insisted Kate.

"Hil-lary?" Gee singsonged. She knew no one could lie to her once she'd asked them directly.

Hillary glanced down at her lap and then back at Gee. She flashed Kate a look of apology in advance and said in a low voice, "Sloan was kind of mean to Kate at clinic."

Gee looked back at Kate with compassion. Kate could tell Gee felt sorry for her, and she was embarrassed. "Why didn't you say anything sooner?" asked Gee. "And why are you insisting nothing happened?"

"I just . . . um . . . Because she's so cool!" Kate finished lamely.

"Oh, here we go again!" said Phoebe, shaking her head and tossing her napkin onto the tabletop in frustration. She rose and began clearing her plate and Gee's. "I refuse to sit through another moment of 'She's cool and I'm not' because it's just ridiculous!" And she stalked over to the kitchen door to deliver the dirty dishes to Sheila.

"What's all this about 'cool'?" asked Gee in confusion.

Kate sighed. She really didn't want to discuss coolness with her grandmother either. How could she begin to explain it? Instead, she decided to just tell Gee what had happened.

"Sloan *was* kind of mean to me at clinic. . . ."

"How?" prompted Gee while her eagle eyes scanned Kate's face for more information.

"Just . . . she said we couldn't ask for donations at certain stores. No biggie."

The screen door to the kitchen swung open with an angry flourish, and Phoebe reappeared. "Did I just hear you say 'certain stores'?! Are you kidding?" She shook her head and pursed her lips. "Try the whole island!"

"Phoebe!" protested Kate. Phoebe smiled at her victoriously and continued to clear the table.

Meanwhile, Gee was distressed. "Oh girls, I am so sorry. Maybe this whole idea of getting the kids to help was a terrible one." She started to rise from her seat. "Why don't I go call the director of the committee and tell her . . ."

"No!" all four girls protested (Kate, mainly because she didn't want Sloan to find out she'd tattled on her — that would mean real trouble), and Gee reluctantly sat back down. "We *want* to do it," said Neeve, and Gee smiled gratefully, knowing that Neeve meant it.

Gee was thoughtful for a moment, and then she said, "Perhaps you should just meet with Sloan and divide up the island? You take half of the places and she takes the other half?"

"That's not fair!" interjected Neeve. "There are four of us and only one of her. We could get things done much faster than she can!"

"Hmm. True. Okay, what if you ask her to list ten places that she wants to herself, and the rest are fair game?"

"No," Phoebe shook her head. "I refuse to submit to Sloan's machinations. Anyway, it's un-American. It's probably even illegal."

As usual, Kate looked inquiringly at Hillary for a translation of Phoebe's grown-up vocabulary, and Hillary shrugged. Phoebe saw them and rolled her eyes in annoyance at their ignorance. "Machinations: her little tricks, her schemes."

Gee tossed her hands up in the air. "Alright then, I guess. Go ahead. I can't think of anything else to suggest. And anyway" — she smiled wryly — "your enthusiasm can only be good for the clinic."

Phoebe folded her arms and smiled in triumph.

But Gee's eyes darkened. "However, you must tell me if Sloan is up to any more of her tricks," she said in a low voice. "And, I suggest that you stay far away from her for the foreseeable future. No sleepovers, no visiting, no hanging out

together. Give each other some breathing space for a while."
The girls nodded in unison.

Now Gee turned back to Kate and patted her gently on the
hand. Kindly, and with great concern in her voice, she said,
"Katie, dear, I'd like to address this topic of people being
'cool' or 'uncool.' I know how important that is to people
your age. Don't get me wrong. But 'coolness' is a terrible
yardstick to measure by. Its definition is always changing with
fads and trends, so it is fleeting by nature. And, most essen-
tially, it is a term that applies to a person's style, and not their
substance or their true worth. There are much better ways to
measure yourself in life."

Gee looked around the table from girl to girl, and Kate
shifted uncomfortably in her seat. "Are you a good person?
Do you have strong morals? Are you kind? Do you treat
people with respect? Do you work hard and meet life's challenges with enthusiasm and pleasantness?" Then Gee smiled.
"And most important of all, do you have confidence in yourself and your abilities, and are you generous enough to share
your gifts with others?"

Kate thought about her gifts and abilities for a moment.
She had decided earlier today that they were useless for someone her age. And the others were going to help her develop
some new gifts. So there was nothing for her to share at this
moment.

Gee continued, "I can practically read your minds: *That's all
well and good but what does this grandmother know about being cool, anyway?*

She's not my age! Well guess what? I was once your age, hard as it is to believe, and I've also had nine children who were all your age at one time or another. And let me just tell you that the things they thought were cool one minute, were not the next. And the people who they thought were cool one year were not the next. So don't go chasing something that is so worthless and slippery. It's a waste of time and energy. Work on the things that matter. And be secure in yourselves, because you're all wonderful people."

The girls were quiet for a moment as they thoughtfully absorbed Gee's opinions — Kate, in particular, was pensive. Gee looked around the table and then chuckled. "Now then. Lecture number fourteen hundred and two is finished. Dessert?"

Dessert was always the highlight of any meal for Kate, but Gee's words still rang in her ears. *Be secure in yourselves.* Hmmm. Maybe the other three could be secure — but for Kate, with her whole image in flux, now was a time of insecurity.

Down at the Dorm that night, the apple-green coffee table was covered with a smattering of papers: Gee's auction catalog from last year, Kate's map of Gull Island, the tiny local phone book, and Kate's To Do book and pink pen. (She had half-hoped to discuss her "New Me" strategies with the others, and parcel out jobs to them, but somehow the topic hadn't arisen, and she was reluctant to bring it up — for fear of what they might suggest.) The girls were each draped over or slumped in the white-canvas-covered couch and club chairs, with everyone but Kate throwing out names of businesses to visit and the various things to ask them to donate.

Phoebe had started the brainstorming with some good ideas. She wanted to get Cabot's to donate a family clambake party, and the Tackle shop down on the dock to donate a year's supply of bait. Hillary suggested a day's boat charter and also bushels of butter-and-sugar corn (that pale yellow and white sweet corn that ripened in August) from the farmer on Huckleberry Lane, and then Neeve had the best one of all: The Town Mayor's parking spot, to be used for a week by the lucky bidder. (The Mayor's office was on Fisher's Path, just outside of town, so many years ago, the town had designated a "Mayor-only" parking spot right in front of the police station — prime town parking on busy days.) The girls howled with laughter at Neeve's brilliance and audacity, and Kate laughed the hardest because, *come on*, no one would ever dare to go ask the Mayor for that. Still, it was a funny idea, and it was then that it occurred to Kate that maybe it *would* be fun if they were all together, going around the island and getting lots of stuff.

Phoebe held on her lap the girls' collective notebook, which they always used for keeping track of their various projects and adventures; she'd been writing down all of their ideas while they brainstormed. Now she read the list back to them, and then grew serious, scoffing that Sloan would probably have locked up the whole town by the time the Callahans set out.

But the others disagreed; it had only been one day, and Hillary pointed out that there were four of them against one of her, so how could she possibly get as much done?

"What do you mean?" asked Kate in sudden confusion. She sat up straight, her shoulders tensed against the understanding that was dawning on her.

"Because when we split up, we can cover four times as much ground as her." Hillary looked at Kate like she was an imbecile.

Kate's heart sank for good. "Wait. *Split up?* You mean we have to get this stuff on our own?!" Panic set in. She'd never thought she'd have to do it all alone! She hardly did anything alone.

"Kate, we can't do it all together," explained Hillary patiently. "We'd never get it all done."

"But . . ." What she wanted to say was that there was no way she could do it alone. Actually, she wanted to scream in terror and cry, begging them to do it as a team. But everyone was looking at her in resignation, as if they could foresee the emotional scene that was coming, and Kate was mortified. So she stopped in her tracks and took a deep breath. If she was going to reinvent herself, the first thing she wanted to do was stop being a crybaby.

"Okay. Fine," she said evenly. Phoebe raised her eyebrows and looked at Neeve, and Hillary smiled in relief. There wouldn't be a scene after all. "Fine," said Kate again, as if trying to convince herself. "I can do that." And she prayed that she could.

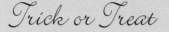

CHAPTER FOUR

Trick or Treat

The girls avoided Sloan at clinic the next day, out of fear or hatred, depending on the girl. But Kate did watch her from a distance. She saw the way Sloan flirted with the boy counselors; she saw how her clothes were up-to-the-minute trendy, and how they hung just right on her whippet-thin frame; and she saw how Sloan's dark tan made the light green of her eyes really pop. She examined Sloan's gold earrings flashing in the light, and her perfect manicure, in contrast to Kate's short, bare nails. She took note of the sinewy muscles that strained in competence when Sloan hefted a boat, and how she easily used one hand to swing a big pile of life preservers back in their bin.

But most importantly, Kate observed Sloan's nonchalance at jumping off the dock and swimming to untie a knot that had accidentally formed between the ropes of two different boats. Kate could never in a million years have jumped into that water. It was deep, and cold, and murky in the shade under the dock, and it terrified her. She wasn't a big water person, anyway, not being brave enough to swim in the ocean on anything but the calmest of days, and disliking the cold water of Gee's unheated swimming pool. *Sloan is brave*, she thought. And then, strangely, *Maybe there are things I could learn from her.* She couldn't quite believe she'd think such a thing, and she didn't dare mention this to the others, but she tucked the idea away, to revisit later.

During break that morning, Kate's following was stunned to discover she hadn't brought snack. They sought her out, as usual, and after some mild ribbing (they didn't believe she hadn't brought anything), the mutiny began. Kate felt guilty at first for her impulsive decision not to bring snack, but then she was annoyed by her guilt.

"Sorry, guys," she announced. "I guess you all have to fend for yourselves today."

"But you do it so well! *'You sweet-talker, Betty Crocker!'*" sang Atticus, an eleven-year-old boy that the Callahans were friends with. Kate cringed at the comparison; Betty Crocker was an old lady. *That* was for sure. And Kate was not.

She huffed indignantly and said, "Why don't *you* bring snack tomorrow, old man?!"

Atticus looked at her in momentary confusion, then said, "Whatever you say, old lady."

Aargh! Kate had no comeback, so she turned away while the crowd grumbled and then dispersed, hungry and empty-handed. She was left wondering if anyone actually liked *her*, or if they really just liked her snacks.

▲

After clinic, the four cousins stayed late at Hagan's and ate a quick picnic lunch packed by Sheila (and carried by Kate, of course): homemade chicken salad sandwiches, potato chips, bread-and-butter pickles, and a Thermos of red Kool-Aid. Then they set out for town, armed with their lists.

They'd divided the master list into four chunks, and then traded stores back and forth between them, in order to play to their strengths. For instance, Kate would hit the Old Mill, the crafts store in town that was her favorite. And Neeve would ask at Booker's, because their friend Talbot worked there and he had a crush on Neeve, so he'd probably make sure they got something good (but first, they waved her off up Fisher's Path, toward Town Hall, laughing at her nerve and wishing her good luck, knowing she'd probably fail in her quest for the parking spot).

Everyone was to meet back at the town park in half an hour for an update. Kate was sick with fear, but she forced a smile on her face, at least while she was with the others, and ignored their inquiring and solicitous looks as she set out on her own. Hillary had privately offered to accompany Kate, at least on her first few stops. But Kate had decided that she had to do it on her own; she couldn't let the others keep living her life for her or she'd never improve. So she'd turned Hillary down with a grateful hug, and steeled herself against the fear that brewed and sloshed inside of her.

Kate had decided that her first stop would be the Old Mill. Her rationale was that she might have success there, since the owner would recognize her, so she'd be able to start out strong. But she dragged her feet after Phoebe and Hillary dropped her at the corner of Broad Street and headed on down Market. She'd waved happily to them until they were out of sight, but inside she was terrified. She'd dressed carefully this morning, in order to look presentable and well-to-do, not like a street urchin begging for handouts (which was what she felt like), and she'd tried writing out a little script and practicing her lines, but they felt stilted and awkward when she'd recited them.

Now, all too soon, Kate had reached the Old Mill. She stood outside, pretending to admire the antique windmill — with its weathered, silver-colored wooden shingles, and its huge spokes, creaking in the breeze — as if she'd never seen it before. Really, she was caught there: too scared to go in, but knowing she couldn't leave. To summon up her courage, she tried thinking of other stressful situations in her life where she'd triumphed, but that backfired; those memories only made her heart beat harder. Finally, she felt too conspicuous to stand outside any longer, and she had to enter.

Inside, the shelves were laden with most of Kate's favorite things in life: jars of colorful beads, rolls upon rolls of decorative ribbons, skeins of gorgeously colored yarns, kids' craft kits, paints, silky sable brushes, cute buttons, and myriad other craft supplies. But she was too nervous to browse, even though she needed needlepoint thread. And actually she felt a tiny bit sad. Kate loved this place and was sorry that she had to taint her feelings for it with this nerve-racking expedition.

With a quick glance, she realized the owner wasn't there; it was just a young salesgirl who'd waited on Kate numerous times. Should Kate leave now? Come back later? Her heart lifted in hope, but no. She forced herself to stay. After all, she'd gotten this far. The girl was busy helping another customer, so Kate stood to the side of the counter to wait, gulping repeatedly to keep her mouth from drying out. Finally, the transaction was complete and the salesgirl turned to greet Kate and ask if she could help her.

Kate's face turned red, and then scarlet, as she became more embarrassed for being embarrassed: a vicious cycle of embarrassment! Finally, she stammered out that she'd like to see the owner. But the salesgirl explained that the owner had gone to the mainland for the day, and offered to leave a note for her.

Relief flooded over Kate like a cold bucket of water. A note! Brilliant! And so much easier than having to ask in person! While Kate said thank you six times, the girl produced a pad of paper and a pen (although Kate had naturally reached for her own in her tote bag), and Kate tried to steady her shaking hand enough to write her request neatly.

When she finished, she smiled so broadly and happily at the

salesgirl that the girl gave her kind of a funny look, but Kate didn't mind now. She was just so relieved to be able to cross one place off her list! The girl scanned the note quickly and promised to get it to the owner as soon as she returned. Another customer was waiting, so with a wave and another profuse stream of thank-yous, Kate turned and left the store, closing the screen door carefully behind her so that the salesgirl would remember her as a conscientious customer.

Outside, she stood blindly for a moment as her eyes adjusted to the bright sun after the comparative darkness of the store. She was breathless with exhilaration. She'd done it! All by herself! It was like swimming a mile in shark-infested waters and living to tell the tale!

But the bliss of success was short-lived, and reality came crashing in as she realized that her next few stops wouldn't be this easy. She had to try at least two more places before she could turn up at the town park and face the others, and she was sure that she wouldn't be so lucky again. Her next stop would be the fabric store, and she didn't have long to compose herself, as it was only next door.

Her feet started walking almost against her will, and too soon, she found herself standing inside the fabric store, which was really just the right-hand side of the hardware store (run by a husband-and-wife team who'd decided to merge their expertise into an old-fashioned dry-goods type of store). Kate had, of course, been there numerous times to buy supplies for herself and for their Dorm redecoration project, and it was a place she felt comfortable in. But as at the Old Mill, she was excruciatingly embarrassed at her mission, and she waited until everyone else had been helped and left the store before she approached the owner.

A kindly compact woman with jet-black hair, dark eyes, and the busy manner of a blackbird, the owner was never still. She folded and refolded bolts of cloth while talking to customers, not even needing to look at the work her efficient hands were doing. "May I help you?" she asked Kate chirpily as Kate slid shyly along the counter.

"Um. Yes. Please." Kate paused. *Oh dear. Where to begin?* "I'm here to see . . . if . . . there's any chance . . . uh, not that you have to, but . . ."

The woman looked at her kindly, with her head cocked inquisitively to the side. Her hands stilled as she watched Kate struggle to get the words out. Kate felt like she was speaking a foreign language, and that the woman couldn't understand a word she was saying. Finally, it all came out in a graceless, unpolished rush.

"There's a benefit for the clinic, with an auction, and a raffle, and it's at my grandmother's house, and she asked us to get donations, so would you, could you, consider donating anything?" There! She'd done it!

But the woman's eyes took on an expression that Kate hadn't anticipated. Once her incomprehension melted away, there was a look of pity on her face.

"Oh, I am so sorry, sweetie, but I already made a donation

yesterday, to the Bickets' daughter . . . ummm, let's see, Sam? Sarah?"

Kate was stunned. She hadn't considered the outcome of her request; success had been assured just because she'd tried. She'd never imagined she'd be denied once she actually got the words out. "Sloan. Sloan Bicket," Kate offered in a voice of defeat. Her heart sank like a stone.

The woman perked up. "That's right! She's in school a couple of years ahead of my daughter. Anyway, I am so sorry, but I did give her quite a nice donation, as it is for a very good cause. But it's good of you to try. I wish I could give more, but as I said, it was quite a lot for me, so . . . good luck to you!" And she picked up the bolt of cloth she'd been straightening, and walked away to reshelf it.

Kate felt, if possible, lamer than ever before, and she walked away as quickly as her feet would decently carry her, without breaking into a run. Sloan had already been there! And the worst part was, the woman felt sorry for her! Kate bolted through the door with a "Thanks!" tossed over her shoulder, since her manners never failed her, even in defeat, and she walked quickly across the street to leave the scene of her humiliation far behind. *Well, that's that*, she told herself sadly. *I'll never be able to go in there again.*

The last thing she ever, ever wanted to do, ever again, was try another store. She resolved as she walked to the corner of Broad Street to turn onto Market, that she'd just get to the park early and wait for the others, whereupon she'd announce that she had retired from the donation solicitation business, and would happily offer to stuff party bags or make herself useful in some other way. She had to preserve the tiny shred of dignity that remained in her, and the only way to do this was to cut her list short and call it a day.

But when she reached the corner, she suddenly caught a glimpse of Phoebe leaving The Pantry with a white envelope in her hand. The owner of the store was standing in the doorway waving and chatting and smiling, and Phoebe was waving and smiling back. Kate caught her breath, drew back before Phoebe could see her, and flattened herself against the cool, scratchy brick wall of the Coolidge House hotel. She was embarrassed that she had nothing to show yet, and Phoebe, clearly, did. Now she didn't know what to do. She felt paralyzed. Should she just throw in the towel, as she'd just been planning? Or should she try one more place, just in case?

Ugh! Kate was frustrated. But now another shopper, a woman Kate's mom's age, was coming along Broad Street, and Kate was embarrassed to be just standing there, plastered to the wall. So she peeled herself away and reached into her bag for her list, to make it look like she was busy (naturally, she'd already committed her list to memory, but still). She scanned it blindly and looked up and down the street. White's Drugstore, she decided. And off she walked, retracing her steps in a haze of nervousness so thick that later, she didn't even remember her short stroll to the store.

CHAPTER FIVE

White's

Kate hefted the shopping basket onto the counter at White's Drugstore and began unloading it for the teenaged checkout girl. Kate had been too nervous to ask for a donation without having bought something first. She figured she'd stock up on a few things, just to show what a good customer she was, before she approached the manager with her request. So she'd picked out items she thought might help her with her makeover, pleased for the few moments of distraction from the donation process. Besides the birthday cards for her friends back home, there was self-tanner, whitening toothpaste, a box of hair dye, a pump dispenser of cellulite cream, and a few other miscellaneous skin potions and cosmetics.

While she waited to be rung up, her stomach did flip-flops of nervousness. To occupy herself, Kate gazed at the tabloid magazines on a rack at the counter.

"Hey, Callahan!"

Kate froze. *Sloan!* she thought. But she didn't want to turn around to make it a reality.

"Callahan!" Sloan singsonged. She sounded closer.

Kate gulped, and then slowly turned around. Why did she always have to be alone when she ran into Sloan?

"Hello? Anybody home?" Sloan now stood right behind Kate and pretended to knock on Kate's head.

Casually, Kate tried to shield her purchases from Sloan, mortified by the array of self-improvement products laid bare on the counter. She braced herself for a withering comment from Sloan that would compound her humiliation. (Oh, why couldn't drugstores be by appointment only, with just one customer at a time?)

"Uh . . . hi, Sloan. . . ."

Mercifully, the cashier handed Kate her change and the bag, and Kate walked quickly to the exit. In her embarrassment, she'd forgotten that she was supposed to talk to the manager. But as she walked away, she remembered why she'd come in in the first place. Drats! Now she was stuck. She didn't want Sloan to watch her ask for a donation, nor did she want to leave without one. She decided she'd go outside for a moment to compose herself, and then return to make the request when Sloan had left the store.

"Hey, so . . . ," Sloan called after her.

"What?" Kate spun around. She would not normally have dared to be this impatient or rude with Sloan, but the combination of her embarrassment at the register and her frustration with Sloan's presence had suddenly made her angry. To top it off, she was mad at herself for not being brave enough to go get the donation in front of Sloan.

Sloan looked a bit taken aback by Kate's rudeness at first, but then something in her eyes shifted and a new look crossed over her face. She suddenly seemed kind of impressed or . . . intimidated, Kate realized in shock. *But how could* she *be intimidated by* me? wondered Kate.

"Oh, nothing. Just . . . see you around," Sloan said lamely.

"Yup, see ya."

Outside, Kate stopped short. She was shaking; she couldn't believe she'd just been rude to Sloan! She almost felt bad; it just wasn't her nature to be mean. But she was still angry, and not just because of the interaction they'd just had. She was mad at Sloan for scaring her at clinic yesterday, and — Kate realized with surprise — she was mad that Sloan had gotten the fabric store donation — that she had beat Kate to it! And now Kate had just left yet another store empty-handed. *Well, you know what?* thought Kate, *the New Me is not going to let her beat me again! I'm going back in there and getting that donation, even if she does watch me do it!*

So she drew herself upright, took a deep breath, and marched right back into White's to get her donation, her anger propelling her like a motor. But as the door hushed shut behind her and the air conditioning swirled thickly around her ankles, she realized her mistake: she never should've left the store. For there ahead of her was Sloan, in animated conversation with the manager of White's.

Kate's anger dissipated, like air hissing out of a popped tire. Her heart sank, and her shoulders sagged in defeat. *Of course*, she thought, as the familiar — even comfortable — sensation of being last in line settled over her shoulders like a cozy, favorite poncho. But as she turned to go, she thought, *Wait just a minute, missy! What would a cooler person do in this situation?* She paused for a moment and then turned back, forcing herself to join Sloan while she talked with the manager.

Sloan was nearly as surprised as Kate by her return, but Sloan smoothly introduced her to Mr. Singh, a movie-star-handsome Indian man with combed-back black hair, dark black eyebrows, and white, white teeth. He bowed at Kate and said in a musical voice that he was pleased to meet yet another one of "Mrs. Callahan's fine grandchildren," then he continued his transaction with Sloan, and Kate stood there mutely. While she waited — doing nothing, saying nothing — embarrassment dampened her new bravery like a bucket of water thrown onto a fire. *What am I doing here? Who do I think I am, hanging around with Sloan Bicket? And why am I just standing here awkwardly, like a lump, not contributing anything to the conversation?* She had been able to imagine someone cooler in this situation, joining Sloan, but she couldn't imagine any further than that. *What should I say? Should I even speak at all?* Kate wished fervently that she was someone else. But she wasn't bold Neeve, or brave Hillary. She was Kate: mild, polite, and chicken.

Sloan and Mr. Singh agreed on the donation of a line of Clinique skin care, as well as a gift certificate to the store, and Sloan shook his hand, agreeing to return to pick up the coupons. Then she deftly maneuvered Kate away from the manager and up to the front of the store, where she stood with her hands on her hips and fire in her eyes.

"What was that all about? Were you trying to horn in on my donation?"

Kate stammered, coming to her senses, as if she'd been dreaming. "I . . . I just . . . I thought I'd get a donation; then I saw you there. So I just wanted to see how you did it." Now that Kate was back to her usual self, there was no question of standing up to Sloan.

"The early bird catches the worm, baby. Anyway, you can't come to this store. It's one of mine."

Kate surreptitiously wiped her sweaty palms down the legs of her shorts, hoping they wouldn't leave a wet trail on the fabric. She was too nervous to look down and check, so instead she stammered, "Uh, um, Sloan, I meant to ask you. How are we supposed to know what stores are 'yours,' anyway?"

"Pretty much any store where I or any member of my family has ever worked, or that we own." Sloan's extended family had a hand in many businesses on the island. "Also any place where my dad or mom is friends with the owners, or where I'm friends with the owners' kids . . ." She was ticking things off on her fingers now.

"Wait a minute. That's not fair! That's practically every store in town!" Kate's innate sense of justice leapt to the surface now, momentarily squashing her fear of Sloan.

Sloan smiled smugly. "So?"

"Well, we don't know all those people. But we can still go into stores and ask!"

"Uh, no. You can't. Like I said, I'm doing it."

"Why do you even care? It's not like there's some sort of a race here. Like, who can get the most stuff." Kate blinked hard and swallowed. She couldn't believe she was actually having a debate with Sloan.

Sloan batted her eyelashes in an annoying way. "Not officially."

"So you're just competing against us?" Kate pressed on in a most un-Kate-like way.

"I'm competing against everyone. Especially summer tourists like you."

"Why?" pushed Kate, pointedly ignoring the "tourist" remark.

"Because I like to win." Sloan turned and stalked out the door.

"Oh." Kate couldn't think of a comeback (*Phoebe would know what to say*, she thought), nor could she just follow Sloan out of the store. So she stood there for a moment more, smiling awkwardly in case anyone had been watching. "I like to win, too, I think," Kate said tentatively to Sloan's back, surprising herself. She wasn't quite sure of it, yet, but the seed of competition had been planted.

She paused for a moment to make sure Sloan was well and truly gone before she exited the store. Then she, too, left, peeking in both directions to make sure Sloan hadn't lingered, wanting to continue their little fight.

Now that the adrenaline had worn off, Kate was knock-kneed with fear. She couldn't believe she'd stood up to Sloan, even for a minute! How dare she?! Weak and trembling, she collapsed onto a park bench at the edge of the sidewalk to re-group. Her bag plunked down heavily next to her, laden with her purchases, as well as her regular gear. She fanned herself in the muggy heat, and reviewed her efforts.

How humiliating: Three stores, and nothing to show for it. And now it's time to meet the others. What will I say? wondered Kate morosely.

CHAPTER SIX

Got It

Kate glanced at her watch as she walked slowly to the town park. Five minutes late, and yet she was dragging her feet, reluctant to meet the others.

Her "New Me" list had said: *Be braver.* But she'd tried being brave and it hadn't worked. So from now on, the only way she was going out again was if one of the other cousins came with her.

At the corner, she could just make out the other three, perched on a bench in the park and chatting animatedly, despite the hazy sky glowing white above them. Neeve seemed to be telling a story, and the other two were laughing. It looked as if they were all happy. As if they'd had fun.

Fun! Ha! thought Kate in disgust. The unfamiliar anger surged again inside of her (was she mad at Sloan? At herself? Both?), coupled with shame and fear. She was miserable. And it must've been written all over her face, for as she neared the others, Hillary saw her and jogged to her side to meet her.

"What's wrong, Katie? Are you okay?"

That little bit of sympathy was all that Kate needed, and the tears began to flow. She'd been swallowing them back a whole day now — ever since this new donation plan had been hatched — and she just couldn't keep it in anymore. In fact, very quickly, she was crying so hard that she couldn't even speak. All of her plans to toughen up were forgotten in her misery.

Neeve and Phoebe were clearly alarmed. They, too, jumped up from the bench and came to her side. Kate tried to catch her breath to tell them that she was fine — it was just that the donation thing had been a bust, but it took a minute before she could calm down enough to tell them. She hated being comforted, instead of being the comforter — it put her totally out of sorts. Finally, she pressed the heels of her hands to her eyes, *hard,* and she stopped. Phoebe, Neeve, and Hillary looked at her expectantly, and she croaked, "I didn't get anything."

"Is *that* why you're crying?" asked Neeve, her dark eyebrows knit in confusion.

Kate nodded mutely.

Phoebe rolled her eyes, and sat back down on the bench. "Phew!" she said. "I thought something bad had happened."

"But it was bad!" protested Kate. "I was mortified! And terrified! I'll never do it again!"

"Okay," said Neeve. The others nodded.

"Yeah, you don't have to do anything that makes you feel uncomfortable," agreed Hillary.

"Why should you? We can handle it," added Phoebe, crossing her long legs comfortably.

Kate looked at them all in surprised confusion and burst into tears again. "But I *want* to!" she wailed. She buried her face in her hands and sat down heavily on the bench next to Phoebe. No one said anything, and when she looked up again, Hillary was shrugging at Phoebe and Neeve's eyebrows were raised so high that they were practically hidden under her hair. For a moment, Kate hated them all. They were so . . . sure of themselves, and smug, and she felt like they were ganging up on her.

"Sorry." Kate reflexively apologized for her tears, and then quickly wished that she hadn't. She wasn't sorry! She was upset and they could very well comfort her. She pulled her handkerchief from her tote bag and dried her eyes and blew her nose. Then she retrieved a little foil packet from her bag, tore it open, and removed a folded face wipe. This she unfolded and blotted all across her blotchy face, then she tucked it in its wrapper, crumpled the little package, and neatly dropped it in the garbage can next to the bench. Next, she took a deep breath, located a Tic Tac box in her bag, popped three green Tic Tacs, shook the box all around to offer it to the others, who declined, and then stowed it away. She tucked her tote bag behind her legs, took another deep breath through her nose, folded her hands on her knees, and sat up straight.

"Okay," she said.

Phoebe smiled. "Are you finished with your ministrations?"

"My what?" Kate looked at Hillary and Neeve, but they shrugged at Phoebe's vocabulary, as usual.

"Your little comforting rituals," said Phoebe, gesturing at Kate's tote bag.

"Oh. Yes," said Kate with a cold glare.

"Okay, so let's get this straight," began Neeve, her hands on her hips. "You don't want to go get a donation ever again. But you do. Right?"

Kate nodded. "I guess."

"What do you mean?" asked Hillary.

"Wait, first of all, what happened?" interrupted Neeve.

Kate recounted her three stops, and the others listened, asking questions occasionally. Phoebe pointed out that Sloan was getting pretty far on her own, so it really *was* good that there were four of them out there, competing against her.

They were silent for a second, and then Hillary said, "Guess what Neeve got?"

"No, Hillary, not now. It can wait," Neeve tried to hush Hillary.

"What?" asked Kate. "Tell me." She felt left out as the others exchanged glances; a smile played on Neeve's lips.

Finally, Neeve said, "I got it."

"What?"

"The parking spot, silly! I got the Mayor's parking spot!"

She jumped up and did a silly little victory dance, while Kate's eyes widened and her jaw dropped.

"No. Way!" breathed Kate. "How?"

Neeve sat back down on the bench and shrugged. "I just asked." She grinned. "And the Mayor thought it was a hilarious idea; no skin off his back. So he said yes!"

"Wow." And then, "Huh. I can't believe you did it." Kate stared at nothing for a minute while she marveled over the fact that she and Neeve were even related. How could one of them turn out so brave and the other so chicken?

"Listen, Kate," Hillary said, "I don't really think that your three tries sounded so bad. You might still get something from the Old Mill. And the fabric store and White's didn't say no, exactly. They just gave the donations to someone else who got there first. Gee even told us that that would probably happen."

It didn't sound so bad when Hillary put it that way, Kate had to admit. Even though *she* had gotten to White's first, actually.

"I guess," said Kate. "It's just that I dread trying again. But I don't want to be left out. And even more, I don't want to . . ." she rolled the phrase around in her mind before she dared to say it out loud. But it sounded okay. "I don't want to be a loser. Like, I don't want to *lose*."

Hillary looked at her seriously. "Can we help you?" she asked.

"Maybe," said Kate. She sat in silence, thinking.

"How?" asked Neeve finally.

Kate collected her thoughts and then said, "First of all, I really want you guys to help me tonight. I want to start my new image and, like I said, I need your help." The others nodded seriously and Kate continued. "And as for the donations, maybe we could try one place all together?" she suggested finally. "Like you could come with me while I ask? And then, maybe give me some pointers afterward if I, like, don't get it?"

"Okay." The others were game.

"But where?" asked Neeve, tapping her lip with her finger while she thought.

"I know!" said Phoebe suddenly. "Let's go to Summer Reading!"

"Oh, but that's your favorite store!" protested Kate. "You should get it! In fact, why didn't you get it already?"

"Don't worry about it. It's just because I wanted to save the best for last. But come on. Let's go see Mr. Bradshaw."

CHAPTER SEVEN

Summer Reading

Kate realized her mistake the moment she entered Summer Reading. *Oh dear,* she thought. *Now the cousins are going to watch me! It's just like White's all over again!* But the bell jingled as the door closed behind them, and the bookstore's proprietor looked up from the paperwork he was doing at the long wooden counter to one side of the large two-story room, and Kate was trapped.

Summer Reading was empty at this hour on a hot sunny day, as almost everyone who was not at work was busy cooling off at the beach or napping in a hammock somewhere in the shade, and the squishy armchairs and ottomans nestled around the bookstore looked invitingly cool and comforting. A loft ran around the perimeter of the second floor, and Kate tipped her head back to take in the shelves and shelves of colorful books lined neatly along the walls. It was a beautiful and welcoming space, with the smell of cinnamon coffee drifting through the air. Kate's senses were instantly charmed, and she felt herself calm down considerably. Maybe she could do it. Maybe. She swallowed hard as the owner greeted her.

"Good afternoon, girls! Oh, and it's Miss Phoebe Callahan! Are these your cousins?" Kate was startled by his greeting. She'd forgotten for a moment that he and Phoebe were so friendly. (Phoebe the bookworm had independently befriended the bookstore owner and the town librarian — the two most literary people on the island — while the others were busy shopping for craft supplies or sporting goods.) The man's eyes were warm and twinkling behind his glasses, and even his salt-and-pepper beard couldn't hide his enormous friendly smile. A trim spotted mutt that had been sleeping by his feet struggled to stand, and then thought better of it. Kate was glad; she wasn't crazy about dogs.

"Hi, Mr. Bradshaw! Yes, these are the illiterate Philistines I've been complaining about."

"Welcome, girls. I'm sure Phoebe is underselling you and that you've all done plenty of reading in your day. Am I right?" Kate and the others smiled and nodded, immediately put at ease by his relaxed and friendly manner. It was the rare adult who could talk to kids as if he understood them without seeming like he was trying too hard to be cool; Mr. Bradshaw was obviously one of them.

He turned back to Phoebe. "So what brings you in on a beautiful beach day like this? Can I help you find anything?"

"Actually . . . ," Phoebe began, and she turned to Kate.

Mr. Bradshaw's eyes followed hers until they, too, came to rest questioningly on Kate.

Kate's mouth went dry and she felt like she was going to throw up. She didn't know where to begin! Summer Reading wasn't one of her usual haunts, and besides being nervous, she felt totally out of her element.

Mr. Bradshaw must have sensed the great anxiety going on inside Kate, because he tapped his hands lightly on the counter, then stood up from his stool and came around to the front. "Follow me," he said, and the four girls (and the dog, who was apparently devoted to Mr. Bradshaw) walked behind him to a special nook in the side of the store, which was hung with signs saying "BIG KIDS ONLY!" "NO TWERPS ALLOWED!" and things like that. Kate smiled and felt herself relax a tiny bit. Why hadn't she been in here yet this summer? She'd been in a few times as a small child, but that must've been before Mr. Bradshaw took over, because all she remembered were piles of dusty used books and a cranky old lady who didn't like children.

The five entered the nook and found a cozy space with huge beanbags on the floor, lava lamps glowing in a corner, a computer station with Internet hookup, and shelves and shelves of brand-spanking-new books just for kids ages ten and up. The dog plopped down again and fell instantly asleep, his nose resting on his paws.

"My kids made me build this addition," said Mr. Bradshaw, laughing. "They complained that they were tired of hanging out with the babies and listening to the moms read *Goodnight Moon* while the toddlers chewed on board books. I happen to love our kids' section, with all its toys and bright colors, but I understood their point. They designed this and picked out all the decorations and even donated some stuff from their own rooms." He gestured to the lava lamps with a grimace. "Not my taste, exactly, but they and all their friends like it."

"How old are your kids?" asked Neeve. But while Neeve was sensing a new social opportunity, Kate's smile had tightened on her face. Sloan's qualifications for banned stores were still echoing in her head, and she just knew Sloan must be friends with Mr. Bradshaw's kids.

"Ten and sixteen. Boy and a girl. They're visiting their cousins in Long Island this week and having a ball, from what I hear." He smiled and folded his arms across his chest. "So was there anything in particular you were looking for? I've got gross books, funny books, princess books . . . ?"

Ten and sixteen might be okay, thought Kate. *After all, Sloan is twelve, so she wouldn't be in the same grade as either of them.* Suddenly, she realized that everyone was looking at her again, including Mr. Bradshaw, who had an expectant smile on his face.

Kate cleared her throat. "Um . . ."

Neeve smiled encouragingly, and Hillary gave her a tiny nudge. Kate didn't look at Phoebe.

"Um . . . you said princess books?" Darn it! She couldn't ask!

"Yup. Right here." Mr. Bradshaw knelt down next to a low shelf that was painted entirely pink. "My daughter's handiwork. Here you go." He handed her two books and stood again. "Why don't I leave you all to it while I go back to my paperwork. Call me if there's anything else you need. Come on now, Champ, you old lazybones." And with a backward wave he and the dog were gone.

"What is your problem?" hissed Phoebe. "He's one of the nicest adults ever! You could ask him for a thousand dollars and he'd give it to you, if he had it to spare! Now he thinks we're all weird!"

Kate tipped her head to one side and looked blindly at the books in her hands. She was mortified. "It's just . . . I don't know what to say. Oh, won't *you* do it, Neeve? You're so good at this stuff!" She looked imploringly at her cousin and clutched the books to her chest like a shield. Her thumb crept up toward her mouth, but she caught herself in the nick of time and bit her thumbnail.

Neeve looked at her, then at Phoebe. Phoebe rolled her eyes. "Oh, whatever! It's not like I care, anyway." She turned to leave the room. "I'm going up to the loft to look at the plays. I don't care who does it. *I'll* do it if you want. . . ."

"No!" said Kate. "No. Just go."

Phoebe shrugged and left the nook.

"Come on, Katie. You can do it!" said Hillary encouragingly.

"I could do it for you if you want, and we could say you did it . . . ," offered Neeve, her palms face-up in the air.

"No, thanks." Kate was weary of the anxiety now. But she couldn't do it, and she was starting to feel mad again. What did it matter, anyway? Why was it so important to be able to get stupid old raffle donations? Was this a life skill she'd need later? And if so, why didn't they offer it in school, along with social studies and geometry? "Just . . . what should I say?"

"Okay. You say 'Mr. Bradshaw, we're going around town asking for donations for the Thomas and Caroline Sheehan Memorial Clinic benefit, either for the raffle or the auction, and I was wondering if there's anything you might be able to donate. It's for a good cause.'" Neeve said it all rapidly in one breath, and tacked a winning smile onto the end as a flourish. Then she held out her hand toward Kate. "Now you try."

"Uh . . . Mr., um, Bradshaw. We're working for a good cause, and it's a raffle. Would you . . . could you . . . ? Oh, darn it! I can't do it!" Kate smacked her forehead in frustration.

"Calm down, now. Try again. Ready? Mr. Bradshaw, we're going around town asking . . ." Neeve recited her monologue again, and again Kate tried and failed to repeat it. Finally, on the third try, Mr. Bradshaw himself appeared in the doorway.

Kate's heart nearly stopped, she was so embarrassed. Her face turned red and her heart resumed beating with a *thunk, thunk, thunk.*

"I don't mean to interrupt, but I couldn't help overhearing my name." He grinned. "I've been looking for a good cause around the island, because I'm itching to make a donation to something. Have you girls heard of anything that might be worthy?"

Neeve laughed, completely charmed, and even Kate managed a weak smile.

"Yes!" said Hillary.

"In fact we have," added Neeve. And she gave Kate a shove to push her in front.

"It's the clinic. The Sheehan Clinic? There's a raffle. And an auction . . ." She trailed off. She still couldn't manage the asking part, and her knees were shaking so hard she felt like she'd better sit down or they'd give out.

Luckily, Mr. Bradshaw didn't tease them further. "I have just the thing!" he said, and the girls followed him as he returned to the counter. He withdrew a box of cards from under the desk and made out a gift certificate in the amount of $250.

"Wow! Thanks!" said Neeve, who was shamelessly peering over the counter to see how much he'd give.

"That's great!" said Kate, now weak with relief that the whole transaction was nearly finished.

He placed the certificate in an envelope, and sealed it with a beautiful sticker depicting a seagull standing on a jetty. Then with his blue pen he wrote "The Lucky Winner" in fancy script on the front of the envelope.

"Here you go!" he said, pushing the envelope across the counter. Neeve went to reach for it, but then she stood back and let Kate take it. Kate smiled at her in thanks, and put the envelope in her tote bag.

"Thank you," she said. Mr. Bradshaw solemnly offered his hand for a shake.

"It was nice doing business with you," he said seriously. Kate giggled.

"Same," she said. And she turned to leave. She couldn't wait to get outside and discuss her victory with the cousins in privacy.

"Phoebe!" Neeve called up to the loft. "Bee! We're leaving!"

"Coming!"

They said their goodbyes to Mr. Bradshaw, and left the store to wait outside for Phoebe. Kate was practically skipping, she was so relieved.

Outside, Hillary high-fived her and Neeve gave her a hug. "Way to go!" she said.

"Thanks," said Kate shyly.

When Phoebe exited the store, Kate proudly held up the envelope she'd retrieved from her bag. "Look!" she said. "I did it! $250!"

But Phoebe wasn't as impressed as Kate had expected her to be. "Well, not really," she said. Kate was taken aback.

"What do you mean, 'not really'?"

"I mean, he offered it to you because he'd overheard Neeve's little speech. *I* could hear every word even up in the loft!" Phoebe wasn't being mean. Just matter-of-fact.

Kate's heart sank. "But I got it."

"If anyone got it, Neeve got it. But whatever. The important thing was that you tried." Phoebe was walking to where they'd stashed their bikes in the rack up the street.

"Bee, she did get it. She's the one he was looking at when he offered . . ." Neeve was defending her, which only compounded Kate's shame.

"You know what, Phoebe? Let's just leave this one. We'll call it Kate's win and leave it at that." Hillary glanced at Kate, clearly hoping there'd be no more tears today.

"Okay. It's no skin off my back." Phoebe shrugged and stowed her tote bag in her bike basket.

Kate fell behind the other three and put the envelope away. Her triumph had so quickly turned sour, and she just wanted it to be over. Phoebe was right. Neeve *had* gotten it.

Well, so much for the donation process, she thought, searching herself for any sign of relief at giving up. But surprisingly, there was none. She was just sad she hadn't been brave enough to do it alone after all.

Kate slowly loaded her tote bag into her bike basket, and backed the bike out of the rack. Why didn't the others have any problems with this? Why was it so easy for them? Were they just confident? More mature? Shameless? And if so, why couldn't Kate be more like them?

She hoisted herself onto her bike seat and began pedaling, trying at first to pedal fast in order to reach the others up ahead, and then giving up. She coasted as she passed the village green with its Lost at Sea monument.

That's how I feel, she thought, full of self-pity. *Lost at sea.*

She was almost through town when something caught her eye. It was an old house, on the corner of one of the town streets, where the year-rounders lived. It had been old and decrepit since Kate could remember. Really pathetic. But now, someone was fixing it up. Kate stopped her bike on the sidewalk to take a look. She was obsessed with those television shows where houses got fixed up, and she loved the "Before" and "After" sections of decorating magazines.

New shingles, she noted. A paint job. Shutters. New landscaping. It looked amazing! And it had been there all along, but no one had noticed it. What did they always say on those shows about houses that got makeovers? Kate thought for a minute. *Oh yes! It has good bones.*

Kate got back up on the bike and pedaled on happily. She loved to see things fixed like that, and made pretty. It lifted her spirits. And now, it renewed her desire to make over herself. Maybe if she fixed herself up, she'd feel more confident, and she'd be able to do all those brave things that the other girls did so effortlessly. Maybe.

Anyway, it would be fun, and she could use some fun right about now.

CHAPTER EIGHT

The Salon

Kate shifted uncomfortably on her bed. Neeve, Phoebe, and Hillary were scrutinizing her so carefully and silently that she felt like she was naked. She cleared her throat.

"So?" she prodded.

"Shh," admonished Neeve from the next bed, where the three cousins were sitting like judges in a contest. "I'm thinking."

Kate sat still again and said nothing.

Finally Neeve turned to Phoebe and then Hillary. "Okay. I'm thinking we update the haircut — something a little more modern and cool." Her hands fluttered in the air, describing the shape she was envisioning. "Then we do some color, just to give it a little liveliness. Make it look hip. Next stop, eyebrows. Those things have got to go. . . ."

Kate's hands flew to her eyebrows in alarm. "Got to go?! You can't get rid of them entirely!"

"No, no," said Neeve condescendingly. She leaned forward to pat Kate soothingly on the leg. "We're just going to thin them out a little. Give them some shape. Make 'em more sophisticated. It's going to look brilliant!"

Hillary said something to Neeve in a low voice that Kate couldn't hear, but she certainly heard Neeve's outraged response. "Of course I have!" said Neeve indignantly. "I've cut lots of people's hair! Don't forget," she added. "I've lived in lots of places where hair salons aren't exactly a dime a dozen."

Hillary nodded. That was true, but it wasn't like they could check out her handiwork for themselves. Kate's hands flew now to her hair and clutched it. "Uh, I'd be willing to entrust the hair part to a professional; under your guidance, of course."

"Nonsense!" said Neeve.

Oh dear, thought Kate. But then, *At least it's easier than getting donations.* She smiled trustingly at Neeve and tried to ignore the nervous butterflies in her stomach.

"Okay, I guess." There was a pause. "So what do I need to do?"

"Scoot off to the shower and come back. We'll be ready for you."

Kate scampered to the end of the loft and showered; then she slathered herself in her new tinted moisturizer and cellulite cream, careful not to tint her thighs or de-plump her face (although she was tempted). Afterward, she hurried down the ladder and into the living room, where the cousins had set up a chair and laid out a comb and a pair of relatively capable hair-cutting scissors that Neeve had located up in the main house.

With trepidation, Kate crossed the room and sat in the chair. Hillary whisked a towel around Kate's shoulders and secured it with a butterfly hair clip. Neeve shooed Phoebe and Hillary away ("No peeking!") and turned Kate to face the wall. Then Neeve stared at Kate, holding Kate's chin in her hand, and tilting her head this way and that.

"Neeve!" protested Kate. This was a little much. Had Neeve seen this in a movie before or something? It was like she was acting out the role of celebrity hairstylist.

"Okay, okay," said Neeve. "Just thought you'd want me to be careful . . . ," she teased.

"I *do* want you to be careful," agreed Kate.

"Well, then," said Neeve. And she picked up the scissors in one hand and the comb in the other. She combed Kate's wet hair, and it felt good. Kate relaxed a bit.

At first, Neeve's cuts were tentative, but then she got into it, and after watching the first few clumps of hair hit the painted wooden floor, Kate finally had to close her eyes. *Well*, she told herself. *It's hair. It will grow back.*

Neeve, meanwhile, was really enjoying herself. The more she cut, the more of a diva she became. "Can we get some music in here?" she barked at one point, early on. Someone quickly complied; and Hillary's iPod began playing loud ska music, the kind Hillary liked to listen to when she ran.

"*Ackee, one, two, three* . . . ," Neeve sang along out loud. Kate was enjoying the music, too, and she hummed since she didn't know the words.

"Kate!" said Neeve suddenly.

Kate's eyes flew open. "What?" she asked, alarmed by Neeve's urgent tone.

"You're humming harmony! That's amazing! How do you do that?"

"I am?" Kate was pleased. "I don't know. It's just something we learned in Glee Club this year."

"You do have a great ear for music," said Hillary from across the room.

"And a great voice," said Neeve jealously. "I am stone-tone deaf."

"No, you're not," said Kate. "You have a very nice voice." But she wasn't really telling the truth. Neeve wasn't a very good singer, but Kate had never realized it before.

"Whatever," said Neeve. "I just like to sing, so I do it a lot. Hey, Bee! Kill the iPod. Let's have Kate sing!"

"Yeah!" agreed Hillary. "Sing us something good."

Without lifting her eyes from the book she was now reading, Phoebe reached back and turned off the iPod. Kate was embarrassed. It was one thing to sing along with the music, or in a group, like Glee Club. But she'd never sung *a cappella* before in front of an audience.

"What do you want?" she asked, closing her eyes. "I'm taking requests."

"How about you start with . . . a little Avril Lavigne?" suggested Neeve, wiggling her hips in anticipation.

Kate hummed a little bit, then began singing the words to the only Avril song she knew.

The others listened, rapt, and at the end, they applauded. Kate opened her eyes, beamed at the wall, and ducked her head modestly.

"Head up!" ordered Neeve. "I nearly cut your ear off!"

"Sorry," said Kate.

Phoebe put down her book. "Another," she said. "How about something classic?" Phoebe was into all this old sixties and seventies hippie music.

So while Neeve snipped, Kate sang, and twenty minutes passed quickly and happily. The other girls were totally impressed by Kate's singing, and Kate was proud. Finally, Neeve interrupted an old Beatles song.

"Hillary. Hair dryer please! And my brush. And gel!"

After Hillary returned from the loft, Neeve scrunched gel through Kate's hair, and blew it dry expertly. Kate was having so much fun, she'd forgotten why she was sitting there. But finally, Neeve announced, "Ta da!" and she told Kate to stand up and face the others. Kate reached up to feel her hair, but Neeve swatted her hand away. "Don't ruin it yet!" she commanded.

Kate stood and turned around. There was a shocked silence as Phoebe and Hillary stared at her.

"What? Is it awful?!" Kate felt her hair now, not caring

what Neeve said, and she was stunned to find that there was not much left. She flew across the room and up the ladder, tore across the loft and into the bathroom, not waiting to hear what the others said.

"Oh . . . my." She stared at herself in the mirror, but it wasn't really her. Could it possibly be? She looked like . . . a boy? A punk rocker? Maybe . . . Neeve herself? Her hair was still longish on top, with the sides a little shorter, and sticking out, flippy. The back was choppy and shorter, too. Kate lifted her hand and ran it over the newly bare expanse of her neck.

The others had run after her, right on her heels, and now they crammed into the small bathroom behind her.

"I love it!" declared Phoebe, smiling. "It looks really beautiful."

"Yeah!" agreed Hillary emphatically.

Kate was speechless. She looked back at the mirror. She wouldn't cry. She'd known what she was in for when she'd let Neeve begin. She turned her head this way and that and took a deep breath, then she ran her fingers through her hair again, and it stood up — like Neeve's — in little waves and peaks that were . . . actually . . . kind of cool, Kate decided. She sucked in her cheeks. She definitely looked older, and her eyes looked bigger. Her eyebrows *were* kind of thick and immature looking, she decided. But that would have to wait.

"It will take some getting used to," cautioned Neeve. Kate looked at her, and she could see fear in Neeve's eyes. *That* was an unusual sight!

She smiled. It was actually really . . . cool! She looked back at Neeve. "Thanks," she said. She reached out to hug Neeve, and caught the look of relief on Neeve's face as she pulled her in. She hugged Neeve hard and Neeve hugged her back.

"I love it," announced Kate.

"Really?" asked Neeve. "Are you sure?" Neeve was so rarely unsure that Kate felt a rush of warmth for her and hugged her again. "I'm sure," she mumbled into Neeve's shoulder.

Neeve pulled away. "So how about the color?"

Kate laughed and shook her head, which felt so light and unencumbered. "Not tonight. Maybe never, but definitely not tonight. I can only take one thing at a time." Kate left the bathroom and headed back downstairs to sweep up her hair.

"What about the eyebrows?" asked Neeve, trailing behind. Her celebrity stylist turn was coming to an end and she wanted to keep it going.

"Soon," said Kate over her shoulder. It felt good to have a little power over Neeve; to have something Neeve wanted and be able to decide when (or if) she'd let her have it. Kate was enjoying herself.

She grabbed a broom and dustpan out of the cupboard in the living room and swept up her hair. Then she went outside and flung it into the air at the edge of the Dorm's little lawn. Birds like to make nests of it, she'd read in *Martha Stewart Living* magazine one time.

"There you go, birdies!" she said quietly. "I don't need it anymore."

When she entered the living room again, Hillary and Phoebe looked surprised. Hillary laughed. "I didn't even know who you were at first!" she said.

Kate smiled. "It's the New Me! Or, the beginnings of the New Me, anyway."

"I like it," said Hillary.

CHAPTER NINE

Ditching

Gee was totally shocked at breakfast the next morning. She came up from her swim and waved casually at the girls as she passed through the kitchen. "Good morning, chickadees! Be right back!" she trilled. But when she reached the door to the back stairs, she stopped, turned around, and came back to the kitchen table, staring intently at Kate the whole way, her jaw hanging open.

Kate grinned self-consciously, and everyone remained silent as they waited to hear what Gee would say.

Gee walked around Kate's chair to get the full effect, then she planted a kiss on top of Kate's head. "I love it!" she announced, and everyone breathed a collective sigh of relief.

Kate glanced at Sheila across the kitchen, who'd also been shocked when Kate had arrived in the kitchen that morning. Sheila winked at her now. "It's better for cooking, I say. Nothin' to bother with!"

"I agree," said Gee. "I love short hair on women. As you can see!"

The girls giggled.

"So who is your, ahem, stylist?" asked Gee, looking from girl to girl.

"It was me," said Neeve.

"Nice work!" said Gee.

"Thanks."

Gee ruffled Kate's hair as she left to go upstairs and change. "People won't know it's you!" she said with a laugh. "If you were ever thinking of robbing a bank, today's the day!"

"I'll have to check my schedule," said Kate, uncharacteristically sarcastic this morning. Gee laughed at her remark and continued on her way.

"Phew," said Neeve, reaching for a croissant and some jam. "I was so nervous I couldn't even eat until I heard what she thought."

"Not a problem for me," said Kate, selecting her second croissant. She was feeling energized today, and bolder than she'd ever felt before. Maybe it was the weight of her hair off her shoulders, or maybe it was because she felt like she was in costume, dressed up like someone else. But she did feel different. In a good way.

Kate didn't feel the usual dread at going to clinic this morning, because it was replaced by a new excitement about her haircut. *Would anyone there notice?* she wondered. So with a new spring in her step, she rose to put a fresh beach towel, still warm from the dryer, into her tote bag, nestling it right next to her pink bikini (just in case she still felt brave later). As she did so, she realized that her new bottle of self-tanner was still in her bag from the other day. It must've slipped out when she dumped her shopping bag into her tote for the ride home from town. She debated running it down to the Dorm, but decided against it, since the others were already tapping their toes, waiting for her at the door. She didn't want to leave it in the kitchen, since she was vaguely embarrassed by the idea of Gee finding it and questioning her, so she sighed and buried it back in her bag.

At clinic that morning, everyone came up to Kate to praise her new hairstyle. She hadn't been unpopular before, just unremarkable; now it was like she was suddenly the queen bee. She'd never realized that so many kids there knew her name! Even their counselor, Tucker, made a big deal out of it — teasing her that she looked like Amelia Earhart, that icon of female bravery (*"As if!"* Kate had joked back). But she felt good. Later in the morning she saw Sloan across the room, and before she could even think twice about it, Kate lifted her hand in greeting. As she did it, she thought, *Who do I think I am, waving at Sloan Bicket?* Sloan paused, and a look of confusion was quickly replaced by a slow smile, and before Kate even had time to regret her own wave, Sloan waved back! Kate wiggled happily on the dock where she was sitting, and wondered if her former longish hair had been holding her back in some mythical way.

After clinic, the girls decided that it was too beautiful a day to stay in town and work: the sky was blue, the sun blazing, and the air was dry and cool, not hot and humid, for the first time in days. So they headed out to Macaroni Beach to eat lunch at The Snack, the open-air fried and frozen food emporium nestled at the head of the dunes there. Kate pulled her bikini bottoms and bandeau top from her tote bag, and before they left Hagan's, she stopped into the bathroom to change into it. She didn't tell the others, because she wasn't sure she'd even take her shirt off. But just knowing it was under there made her feel good. It was a baby step in the right direction.

The ride to Macaroni took them back toward the center of the island, along the wide-open Fisher's Path, and then onto Huckleberry Lane, the narrow road that lead to Macaroni Beach. The heavy foliage of the tall trees on either side of the beginning of the lane met to form a shady canopy overhead, and the deep green leaves ruffled in the breeze, showing their silver undersides when the wind twisted them. The smell of the ocean was blowing strong today — briny and seaweed-y, as if a heavy tide had washed up lots of sea junk on shore. And sure enough, as they drew near the beach, they could hear big break-ers crashing with a heavy *thunk* right onto the shore. *No swimming for me today,* thought Kate decisively. Not that she ever really swam at Macaroni; she hated waves and much preferred to swim on the sound side of the island, near Gee's house. The only way

she'd ever go in the water at Macaroni was if it was dead calm —
almost oily looking in its shifting stillness; unfortunately, she
then spent her whole time watching the horizon for signs of a
shark fin (which appeared maybe once every third year or so,
and never when Kate was there), and gasping at every shadow
on the ocean floor, until she finally had to jump out, weak-
kneed, and run to the safety of her beach chair.

The girls burst out of the shaded part of the lane and passed
the farm — potato plants and the famous butter-and-sugar
corn growing in neat rows, nearly shoulder-high to the girls
and with fluffy brown silk exploding out of the top of each
stalk. A red Case tractor was parked at the edge of the field,
near the corn, and a covered trailer held a bounty of produce
for sale. The farmer lounged in the shade, tipped back in an
old lawn chair, reading a paperback novel, his boots propped
on the side of the stand. Hillary called to the cousins that she
was stopping to get a donation.

Intrigued, Kate huffed up and pulled over to join her,
while Neeve and Phoebe called back that they'd meet them up
at The Snack.

"Hello!" called Hillary as they leaned their bikes up against
a tree and walked toward the farm stand.

The man tipped his chair down so that all four feet were
back on the ground, then he laid his book aside. "Hello,
there! What can I do ya for?" he asked, smiling.

At first, Kate was automatically nervous on Hillary's behalf.
What if she failed? But she was quickly impressed by how

calmly and smoothly Hillary negotiated the transaction. She exchanged one or two pleasantries about crops and weather, explained to the farmer why they were there, and then suggested the corn donation to him. That was all.

The farmer rubbed the silver stubble on his chin, and thought for a moment. "A'yuh, I could do that. Jest tryin' to think if that's enough," he said.

Hillary glanced at Kate with a smile and a gleam in her eye. They were going to do even better than she'd hoped! Kate smiled back encouragingly. She was surprised that Hillary hadn't felt like she had to buy something before she made her request. Kate made a note of that, and also Hillary's admirable directness and lack of shame. Hillary wasn't pushy or greedy, or even flattering and smarmy; she just spoke plainly, simply, and honestly, and she was clearly a fan of the product she was requesting.

While Hillary and the farmer negotiated the details, Kate inspected the produce for sale. Everything was organic, and maybe because of the warmth and wetness of the summer to date, all of the produce looked lush and delicious. Kate wasn't a big fan of fruits and vegetables, but a sampling bowl of juicy tomato chunks under a glass dome (to keep the bugs away) looked so tempting, she had to try it.

"Mmm!" she said aloud, not able to help herself. The farmer laughed and came to stand by her.

"Aren't they just? I love 'em myself, with a little butter and salt on white bread. Or in a tomato pie that my wife bakes up. Did you try this?" He led Kate to a small section of baked goods she hadn't noticed, on the end of the cart, and lifted the lid on a cake stand. Inside were slices of some kind of a small loaf of bread or cake.

"Try one a these," he offered.

Kate smiled at him in thanks and selected a small slice. The bread was dense and moist, almost like pudding, and it had a ripe sweetness she couldn't place.

"Zucchini bread," he said, smiling. "Ya wouldn't a guessed it, wouldja?" He chuckled. "My wife's a genius at healthy food, ever since I had a heart problem a few years back. Now everything's got vegetables in it, and low fat, and low sodium and all, and I'll tell ya, we've never eaten so well, even bein' farmers and all! I've lost fifty pounds in the past three years!" He laughed and gestured for Hillary to try the bread, then he picked out a slice for himself and munched it thoughtfully, looking out over his acreage. Kate noticed now that all the baked foods were fruit or vegetable-based, and included pumpkin cookies, corn muffins, and fruit pies.

The farmer talked on. "Yep, a lotta changes for us these past few years. Nature conservancy beggin' for the land to be preserved; kids makin' me go organic — that's an expensive thing to turn to, but worth it after the first few years a'hard work. Then my own health problems and the new menu." He turned back and smiled brightly at Kate and Hillary. "Best years a'my life so far, I tell ya! Change is good! Good for the soul." Then he pounded his chest with the end of his fist, "and good for the ticker!"

He walked back to the other end of the stand and began fussing with his reading glasses and some paperwork. "Now let's sort you out over here and get you on your way. No need to go listenin' to an old man all afternoon when ya could be down havin' fun at the beach."

Hillary finished the transaction while Kate helped herself to another little slice of zucchini bread. She couldn't believe it was made with vegetables, and organic ones to boot! She'd have to look into a recipe like that. Maybe even see if the farmer's wife would share it for Kate's journal. That would be good.

A few minutes later, they joined Neeve and Phoebe up at The Snack. Kate ordered her usual fried shrimp basket, with a side of fries and a chocolate milk shake, plus a plate of big, chewy ginger snap cookies to share with the others after lunch (*ginger's a plant, too!* Kate noted proudly). Then, careful to avoid splinters, she sat on the wooden picnic bench under the umbrella to wait for her order, and watched the huge waves rolling in. Some daring guys were even trying to surf, but from what Kate could see, they weren't doing too well. *Why would anyone ever think that was fun?* she wondered with a minute shake of her head. *Risking your life, getting tossed around and mashed head-first into the sand, just for the hope that you might get one decent thirty-second ride? Nuts!* She was definitely *not* a water person.

Their lunches were ready, and the girls collected them from the counter, returned to their table, and dug in, chatting while they ate. Neeve was all atwitter about a cute new guy who'd joined clinic, and Hillary was happily discussing with Phoebe a new move she'd learned in sailing that was so complicated and boring Kate didn't even try to follow what she was saying. It wasn't like it was information she'd ever need herself. She zoned out and ate her food and mentally reviewed the New Me list she'd made the other day.

"Makeover," she'd written first. Well, that was under way. She'd gotten the haircut, and had been using the creams and the new toothpaste. Now she just needed to do her eyebrows, try the self-tanner, maybe let Neeve help her color her hair, and get her ears pierced somehow. (How?) She'd also listed new interests — but that was sort of like homework, not that fun — so she set that aside. She was wearing the bikini at this very moment. So that left being braver and getting in shape. She needed Hillary's help for those.

"Hill?"

"Hmm?" Hillary was eating her veggie wrap.

"Remember how you said you'd help me get in shape? And, like, be braver?" Kate picked at a ginger snap while she spoke, absentmindedly sprinkling the crumbs into her mouth.

"Uh-huh."

"When can we start?"

Hillary jerked her head toward the ocean as she finished chewing. "Right after lunch," she said. "I'll take you in."

Kate gasped. "Today? I could never!"

Hillary thought for a second. "Okay, well, then, the getting in shape part we could start." She looked pointedly at the remains of Kate's lunch.

Kate looked down at her empty fried food basket, the dregs of her soda, and the cookie plate. "What?"

"You eat so poorly! Not just that it's fattening, 'cause that's not so important. It's just that you don't nourish your body at all, eating all that junk all the time. Your poor muscles don't stand a chance!" Hillary looked at her sympathetically.

Kate was surprised. "Okay. So what do I need to do?"

"Cut out the junk. The sweets. Eat lots of whole grains, lean protein, and fruits and veggies."

"When would I start?"

"Like I said, no time like the present!"

Kate was taken aback. "B-But . . . ," she stammered. "I was thinking of, like, making a list, and getting . . ."

". . . organized!" the other three chimed in together. Then they fell about laughing and high-fiving each other.

Kate crossed her arms and pouted. "Well, it's important to be organized, you know!" she said indignantly.

"We're just teasing," said Neeve gently.

"It's just that you're so predictable!" said Phoebe, wiping tears of laughter from the corner of her eye.

"Predictable about what I say or what I do?"

"Um, both," said Neeve.

"Like, what do I say that's so predictable?"

"Oh dear!" said Phoebe.

Hillary and Neeve laughed. "Yeah, and *'truth be told,'*" added Hillary.

"*'Heavens to Betsy!'*" said Neeve.

"*'Hillary, do you have your sunscreen on?'*"

The others were roaring with laughter again, and Kate waved her hands to make them stop. "Okay, fine. Just fine. I get the picture. But what do I do that's so predictable?"

"Um, eat food that's bad for you," said Hillary. Kate grimaced.

"Get organized," offered Phoebe.

"Get scared. Fuss over us. *Cry*," said Neeve.

"Knit. Bake. Paint. Chicken out," added Hillary.

"Well, I guess I know what you really think of me, now." Kate huffed and folded her arms.

"You're the one who asked! You're the one who wanted to know how you were predictable!" protested Neeve.

"Well maybe I used to be predictable, but . . ." Kate was about to announce that she was wearing a bikini, but she was interrupted by the arrival of Lark and Sloan beside their table. She squinted up at them, having a hard time seeing their faces with the sun beating down behind them, and her pulse quickened. *Oh dear. What now?* she wondered, forgetting Sloan's friendly wave this morning.

"Hello, Callahan cousins," drawled Sloan. "Long time, no see." She was wearing a blindingly white bikini with little turquoise beads outlining the edges. It was clearly not a suit for swimming. Her dark tan was emphasized by the whiteness of the bikini, and by the frosty pink lipgloss she had on. (*Makeup at the beach?* thought Kate fleetingly.)

"Hi," added Lark, demonstrating a rare ability to speak while Sloan was around. Lark had on a blue bikini, but it was much tamer than Sloan's.

"Hello, ladies." Neeve, the cousins' unofficial spokesperson, smirked. "Nice bathing suits. What brings you here today?" Even though the cousins liked Lark, it was hard to be friendly to her when she was hanging around with Sloan.

"The usual . . . ," began Lark.

Sloan flashed her an annoyed look and interrupted. "A date. With boys. We're meeting them down there in a little while." She waved airily toward the beach. Lark looked at her in surprise and confusion.

"What are you doing? Asking them for donations?" Phoebe could be so condescending when she was mad.

"I do have a life, you know," said Sloan snottily. "But I will say I'm glad to see you're not out pounding the pavement, stealing my vendors out from under me. . . ."

Phoebe started to reply, but Neeve put a calming hand on her arm. Kate knew Neeve didn't want to get into a whole fight with Sloan and have Sloan try to ban them from the donation drive.

"So who are the lucky guys? Anyone we know?" asked Neeve in a voice laced with sarcasm. Kate glanced at Neeve in confusion. Why was she talking like that? Did she think Sloan was lying? Why would Sloan have to lie about meeting boys?

"Uh, no," replied Sloan. "They're older. Like, much older." Lark looked away uneasily. "So, what are *you* doing here?" asked Sloan, turning the tables.

"What does it look like?" asked Phoebe.

Sloan ignored her and changed the subject abruptly. "Hey, what's up with you girls never wearing bikinis, anyway?"

"Oh, here we go again," muttered Phoebe. When the cousins had slept over at Sloan's earlier in the summer, they'd had a big to-do about tanks vs. bikinis.

Before Kate had a chance to speak up about her suit, Neeve piped in, "Why do you care what we wear, Sloan?"

"I don't. It's just that if you would make a little effort with yourselves — acted a little cooler — you wouldn't always be stuck just the four of you. Get it?"

Kate nodded without realizing it. She did get it. But then she caught Phoebe staring daggers at her, and even Hillary looking at her like she was crazy. She stopped nodding and forced a frown of confusion onto her face.

"Has it ever crossed your mind that we enjoy one another's company?" asked Phoebe witheringly. But Kate was suddenly annoyed by Phoebe's rudeness. After all, Sloan was only trying to help them, socially. And it did get kind of old sometimes, just the four of them hanging out together. It's not like they were friends, anyway. They were related! They had to hang out together!

Kate found her voice. "We *could* use some new friends," she stated, looking around defiantly at the others. *Some new friends who don't tease me all the time for being predictable and an old lady,* she added silently. But beneath her calm exterior, her heart was beating rapidly in her chest. She couldn't believe she was taking Sloan's side against the cousins! What was she thinking? She ruffled her new hair in a gesture of uncertainty that belied the confidence in her voice.

But Sloan quickly agreed, and Kate found herself beaming, basking in Sloan's approval and pleased that Sloan had singled her out once again.

"My point exactly," said Sloan. "It's about time you branched out and stopped always hanging around together all the time." Kate nodded again, this time not even looking around to see what her cousins' reactions were. *Who cared if they wanted to just be losers and only hang out with their relatives?* thought Kate, neglecting to realize that Neeve was amazing at meeting new people and just happened to hate Sloan.

Sloan went on, gesturing to Kate. "At least Kate here has taken some initiative and given herself an exciting new look." Kate's heart leapt at the compliment. She couldn't even believe Sloan actually used her name, let alone liked her haircut. A warm flush of happiness and gratitude spread over Kate.

"I'm wearing a bikini, too!" she crowed. The others stared at her. *Well, I am,* she thought.

"Glad to hear it. Anyway, if any of you would like to mingle with cute boys with us," continued Sloan, "then come on down." And she sauntered away, heading for the stairs that led off the deck at The Snack, and over the dunes to the beach below. Kate couldn't decide what to do: should she stay or go? She was reluctant to do either. She did love her cousins, and they were safe, but there was so much she could learn from Sloan; and Sloan *had* singled her out. Lark hesitated, too, and seemed to want to talk to the Callahans.

"Lark!" barked Sloan, turning back when she realized her little deputy wasn't following behind as usual.

But anger flared up in Lark's eyes. "I'll meet you in a minute. I'm hungry!" she called back, with an unprecedented edge in her voice. "Do you mind if I get lunch and join you?" she asked the cousins shyly.

"Be our guest!" said Neeve generously.

"Food is for wimps!" Sloan called over her shoulder. But she was so far away that the statement had little impact among the five girls. Except for Kate. She thought of Hillary's advice, and what the farmer had said. *Food isn't for wimps*, she corrected Sloan silently. *But maybe junk food is.* She pushed her tray away, working hard to ignore the tasty little piece of Bazooka bubble gum that The Snack gave away with each order. Then she took a deep breath and summoned all of her courage.

"I'm finished. I'm going down there." She rose to her feet, and ignored the wobbly nervousness in her knees as she stood. Meeting cute boys and making a new friend were cool things to do, and Kate was going to do both, darn it! Sloan seemed to like her suddenly, and Kate wasn't going to waste this opportunity or let the others hold her back.

Her cousins looked at her, rendered speechless by her act of independence. Even Lark was surprised, but Kate didn't care. *I'm tired of being predictable and safe,* she thought. *It's time to do something different. Something that no one expects!*

Phoebe found her voice first. "You're not seriously going down there to hang out with Sloan?" she asked in shock.

"In a bikini?" added Hillary, astounded.

"Why not?" Kate shrugged, with more bravado than she felt. She picked up her tote bag, looped the handles over her shoulder, and climbed over the picnic bench to leave. *I can't believe I'm doing this, I can't believe I'm doing this,* she thought.

"Oh, let her go," snarled Neeve, who was now mad at her, too. "She'll be the one who suffers for it. Just you watch."

"Katie . . . ," began Hillary, a frown of concern wrinkling her brow.

"Later!" Kate waved breezily. If she stopped now, the fear would take over and she'd miss out on an adventure and on the self-improvement that would come with it. She walked quickly across the deck to the stairs before Hillary could finish, or before she could change her own mind.

CHAPTER TEN

Ditched

"*H*ey," said Kate, trying to control the nervous quiver in her voice. She plopped her bag down next to where Sloan was lying on a towel on the beach.

Sloan half-rose from her supine position and squinted at Kate. "Hey!" she said in surprise. Then she composed herself and asked Kate nonchalantly, "What's up?"

Well, I'm in it now. I'm just going to go for it, thought Kate.

"Nothing," she responded in a level voice that belied her quaking insides. "I'm just a little sick of those guys; they can be so babyish after a while. And I need a little more action, y'know?" She was pleased at how this had come out, but it wasn't exactly true. Or it hadn't been, until now. She felt like she was acting a part; pretending to be someone else. But it wasn't as scary as she'd thought it would be. It was actually kind of fun.

"Yeah, totally," agreed Sloan. "Lark can be so babyish, too. I keep telling her she's got to lighten up, have a little fun. I mean *come on*, we're almost teenagers. Life's too short to act like a loser."

"Totally," said Kate. She spread her towel out next to Sloan, since it was now clear that she was joining her. Inside, she was praying that Sloan wouldn't bring up the whole donation thing again; she couldn't fight that fight right now, not when she still wasn't sure of herself in that arena. So without saying more, she sat on her towel and eased out of her shorts, until she had just her bikini on. She was about to reach for a sarong to wrap around her waist, and then she decided it would look dorky, being too covered up. So she left it in the bag and self-consciously perched on her towel. Because of her easily burned skin and her skin cancer fears, Kate wasn't a sun-worshipper, and she hated lying down on the beach. She preferred to sit and needlepoint or knit. She reached into her bag to grab a sweater she was working on and nearly jumped out of her skin when she heard Sloan's shriek.

"What the heck is that?" Sloan cried when she saw what Kate was holding.

"What? This?" Kate held up the half-made sweater in confusion, and Sloan nearly dove on top of her to hide it.

"Put that away!" ordered Sloan, looking around to see if any of the nearby beachgoers had seen the knitting.

Kate followed the order, losing a row and a half of beautiful stitches in the process. But she still wasn't sure why Sloan was freaking out.

"You. Don't. Knit. On. The. Beach," hissed Sloan. "Or anywhere in public for that matter. Are you crazy? Do you want people thinking we're some kind of old ladies over here?"

Kate cringed at the "old lady" comment. "I hadn't ever thought about it that way before."

"Well, think about it now," said Sloan unkindly. "Especially when you're with me. God!" Sloan shivered in revulsion. "Knitting is for losers."

"Sorry," murmured Kate. What she was exactly sorry for, she wasn't sure. But she didn't want to make Sloan mad this early into their new friendship, if that's what you could call it. And she sure didn't want Sloan thinking she was an old lady, too. Or a loser!

"For a New Yorker, you really are clueless," said Sloan, her eyes wide with wonder.

"Well, I'm not really from New York. I mean not the city, anyway. I'm from right outside . . . ," she began.

"What do you mean?" Kate looked at Sloan and could see distaste in her expression. Uh-oh. Sloan had clearly thought she was hanging out with a sophisticated city slicker, and not just a normal suburban girl. Kate backpedaled.

"Uh, I mean, my dad works in the city, so I do go in a lot. Every week, actually," *Almost,* Kate rationalized in her mind.

I do go almost every week. Or month, anyway. "I mean, I practically live there. I was born there. And I lived there until I was three." She didn't mention that she mostly went in to go to the museum with her mom; that sounded decidedly uncool.

Sloan's expression was softening, and she was nodding. She wanted Kate to be from the city, so she was willing to believe whatever Kate told her.

"In fact, my parents *have* been talking a lot about moving back in soon, now that it's nearly time for me and my younger sister to go to boarding school." Well, they had mentioned it once. Kate's mom wasn't wild about the idea, but it had been mentioned. And her sister wouldn't even be old enough to go to boarding school for another five years. But so what?

Sloan actually looked impressed. "Boarding school? Wow. That's . . . Are you scared to go?"

Kate ruffled her short hair with a confidence she did not feel. "Scared?" she scoffed. "Nah. I'll probably go where my older brothers go. I'm up there all the time anyway. I know practically half the school as it is." In fact, Kate had never wanted to go away to school. Her parents had said they'd take her to look wherever she wanted, but that she shouldn't feel pressured to go, just because her brothers had wanted to. But for a homebody like Kate, boarding school sounded like torture. *Where would you cook?* she always wondered.

"Are the guys cute up there?" asked Sloan eagerly.

"Oh, yeah. For sure," said Kate. She hadn't really thought about it too much since most of them were so much older than she. But she decided to talk it up a little, realizing how cool it made her sound.

Kate's confidence grew as she filled Sloan in on the myriad cute guys at Brooks's and Ned's school. Sloan was dying for details and asking all kinds of questions, and Kate was actually having fun. It was refreshing to be with someone who hadn't known her since the minute she was born (like her cousins), or since preschool (like all of her friends back home). And it felt good to portray this image of herself, even if she was playing up a tiny facet of her life as though it were central to her very existence. She liked this new version of herself, in which she hung out with high school boys and had dinner with them and her brothers in the city (omitting the presence of her parents and her eight-year-old sister, Julie). As she talked, she formed little piles of sand with her hands, sifting its warmth through her fingers, as if she were baking tiny fairy cakes.

Time flew and soon, as she began to run out of her own material, Kate had a question for Sloan. "So where are those guys you were meeting?" Kate looked around, as if they might have been right nearby, hiding under a beach umbrella. Not that she actually wanted them to show up. In fact, she dreaded such a thing. What would she say? What would they think of her? But she did still have the tiniest seed of doubt, planted by Neeve, that Sloan was telling the truth. And she wanted to know for sure.

"Oh . . ." Sloan looked at her watch. "They had work, and they were hoping to get out in time to come down here between shifts. But . . . you know. There was probably a big rush and stuff."

"Where do they work?" asked Kate. Maybe they *were* real. Ha! That would show Neeve!

"Um." Sloan paused, and Kate's suspicion was aroused again. "Coolidge House," said Sloan. It had seemed to Kate that Sloan was trying to name a place that Kate might not go to, and she had thus picked the island's fancy hotel in town.

As a test, Kate said, "Oh, we were just there with Gee. With my grandmother, I mean." She was so used to being with the cousins that she felt funny explaining who Gee was. "What do they look like?"

"Oh, well . . . um. Mark. He's one. He's tall, with, um, black hair. And, um . . ." Kate couldn't tell if Sloan was talking about real guys whom she just didn't actually know, or if she was making the whole thing up entirely. Either way, Kate relaxed a little, realizing that there wouldn't be any social interaction with "older boys" required of her today. Sitting here alone with Sloan was enough work, and taxing enough on her nerves, without adding teenage boys to the scenario.

But much to Sloan's apparent relief, they were suddenly interrupted by Hillary, standing a few yards away, near the foot of the staircase, as if she didn't want to come too close.

"Kate?" she called. "I thought I should come tell you that we're leaving. Neeve and Phoebe are ready to go to town. So . . . okay?"

Kate was paralyzed for a split second. She was supposed to

be going with them, even though she was terrified of asking for more donations. But Hillary was acting kind of weird. Almost like she didn't know her that well, which was very strange, considering that they were cousins and had already spent nearly half the summer together. Anyway, it was exhilarating to conquer her fear and hang out with Sloan. Plus she was learning stuff, like not to knit in public.

"Okay!" Kate called back. "I'll go another time."

"So . . . you're just staying?" asked Hillary in surprise.

"Yeah?" replied Kate, in a "you've got a problem with that?" kind of tone.

"Oh. Fine, then. Whatever. See ya." Hillary spun on her heel, obviously offended, and walked back up to the others.

Kate's body tingled with fear and shock as she watched Hillary walk away. Oh dear. What had she just done?

"See? That's part of your problem right there," said Sloan, jogging Kate out of her trance.

"Huh?" asked Kate, turning back to Sloan.

"Well, you girls are always rushing off together, and being so exclusive. It's like, hel-*lo*? Are you too good for the rest of Gull Island? Aren't we cool enough for you or can you only hang out with each other in, like, your big North Wing palace?" The houses in North Wing were all fancy vacation houses, and Gee's was the biggest and, um, fanciest.

Kate was speechless. Was this what Sloan thought of them? Did everyone else think it, too? The kids in clinic? The kids they'd met through their friend Talbot?

Sloan seemed to realize she'd said too much — not that she seemed worried that she might have offended Kate; just that she might have given away her own insecurity too easily. Kate's embarrassment was turning to a kind of giddy relief.

"People think we're exclusive?" she asked incredulously.

"Well, some people. Not me. I've got better things to do than worry about you and your cousins," said Sloan in a voice dripping with sarcasm. She'd gotten ahold of herself again, and wasn't about to slip up anymore.

"Huh," said Kate. But her mind was reeling. People thought they were cool, but maybe that was just because Neeve was cool, and people assumed that if she hung out with the other cousins, then they must be cool, too.

"Hey, how come you're so pasty?" Sloan interrupted Kate's thoughts again. She was clearly trying to maintain the upper hand; any time her veneer of superiority cracked, she had to do or say something kind of mean to patch it up.

"Oh, I don't tan well. In fact," Kate glanced at her delicate wristwatch. "I need to load up again on the sunscreen." She reached into her bag to get it and simultaneously realized it wasn't there. She gave a good feel around for it, hoping against hope that what she already knew was not true. She'd lent it to Hillary at clinic that morning, and she hadn't gotten it back. Usually it wouldn't have mattered, since the cousins were really never apart. But now it did.

"Uh, you don't have any sunscreen by any chance, do you?" she asked Sloan.

"Sunscreen!" Sloan scoffed. "Sunscreen is for losers. Once you're tan enough, like me, you don't even buy the stuff."

"Well, we have very different kinds of skin," Kate pointed out. Sloan's olive skin was what made her tan so even and dark. All this sun would catch up with Sloan later in life, but right now it looked good. "I wish I could get tan like you," Kate admitted, examining her pale white skin and sprinklings of freckles.

Sloan looked at her with pity. "All you have to do it burn really well a few times, and after the blisters pop, you'll get a really good tan. That's what my friend Cynthia did, and now she tans great, like me."

Blisters! Gross! "That's not really, um, my approach. I'm kind of a wimp about pain," said Kate. It was probably her own hypochondria at work, but now that the allotted time had expired on her first coat of sunscreen, she could feel the sun baking her shoulders and her nose.

Kate dug around in her bag some more, willing the sunscreen to magically appear. Her heart lifted when she felt a bottle, but when she pulled it out, it was only the self-tanner.

"There you go!" said Sloan, peering at the bottle.

"Oh. Can this stuff work as sunscreen?" asked Kate.

"It's better than nothing, if you're going to go all lobster red," said Sloan in disgust.

"Hmmm." Kate examined the self-tanner. NOT FOR USE AS SUNSCREEN, it said in big blue letters across the front of the bottle. She lifted it and showed the bottle to Sloan.

"Oh, that's what they all say. Anyway, if you're going to get fried, you might as well try some. And after the red fades you'll have a good tan underneath from the cream, right?"

It did sort of make sense. Anyway, Kate's only other choice was to go back to Gee's or to town, and it was too soon to do that; it would look like she'd changed her mind about staying and was just chasing the cousins down.

Kate flipped the bottle over and began to read the directions, saving the warnings — her favorite part — for last. Her hypochondria, paranoia, and love of recipes combined to make such reading essential and even enjoyable. But Sloan interrupted her.

"You're not seriously going to read the directions on that thing, are you?"

"Yeah . . . ," said Kate tentatively.

"Just wipe the stuff on. What else is there to it? Slather up!"

"But what about the warnings?" asked Kate.

"Warnings! Are you nuts? Warnings on a cream? Come on! Lighten up! Live a little! What could a cream possibly do to you? God! So paranoid!"

Kate cringed. It was true, what Sloan was saying. What *could* a cream do? And more to the point, she did need to lighten up. Just embrace her fears again, like she'd done when she left the cousins and followed Sloan down here in the first place. Why stop now?

Speaking of which: "Hey, where should I go to get my ears pierced?" she asked Sloan casually. "I want to do it next week."

"Your ears aren't pierced?" Sloan scrutinized her. "Huh. Well, you should go to Gullboutique. It's the only place that could do it right on the whole island."

"Okay," Kate nodded. She cracked open the seal on the self-tanner bottle and poured a big handful of pale pink lotion into her cupped palm.

"Unless you want me to pierce them for you," offered Sloan, not meeting Kate's eyes.

Kate's hand froze in midair, and the self-tanner quickly threatened to leak through her fingers. The idea scared her to death, *and* grossed her out. But she didn't want to brush Sloan off too quickly, for fear that Sloan would never speak to her again.

"Uh, thanks. I'll think about it." Then she quickly slathered the self-tanner up and down one arm, then the other, and, working quickly, soon covered her whole body with the sweet-smelling liquid.

"Ah." She wiped her hands and laid back on her towel, the ocean breeze cooling her all over as it dried the wet cream. Her sensation of being sunburned had subsided, so maybe there was some sort of sunscreen in the stuff. Ha!

Sloan had apparently drifted off to sleep, and Kate was soon half-snoozing, too. Lying in the sand, with a cool new friend, all on her own, with self-tanner doing its magical work: Kate felt good. Not scared at all, actually. And she promptly fell asleep.

CHAPTER ELEVEN

Orange

Kate shivered. Then she sat up in a kind of groggy shock. Where was she? Oh dear. Still at the beach. She'd fallen into a sound sleep and had completely lost track of time. She blinked her eyes, licked her dry-as-a-bone lips, then turned to look at Sloan next to her. But Sloan was gone. *How rude! She didn't even say goodbye. And she just left me here!* thought Kate. *My cousins would never do that,* she added mentally before she could stop herself.

The sun was at a steep angle, and Kate glanced at her watch. Six o'clock! *Oh deary dear!* She jumped up from her towel, threw on her shorts, and hastily tossed her things into her tote bag. She couldn't believe she'd stayed so late! What must the others be thinking right now? She looked around as she hustled up the stairs to the parking lot. The beach was nearly deserted of sunbathers and swimmers, but two young families were now struggling down to the beach with their picnic dinner. *Heavens to Betsy! Gee must be worried sick about where I am!* thought Kate.

She jumped onto her bike, slung her bag into the basket, and began pedaling furiously home. As she rode, the enormity of what she'd done began to sink in. She'd ditched the cousins! It was unthinkable! What had come over her? She bit her lip in shame and tried to think up excuses for her behavior:

I wasn't myself.

I was on a sugar high from the cookies.

It was a joke, and you fell for it! As if I'd ever be friends with Sloan!

But none of it sounded believable. She'd done something really bad — something she never would've believed she could do. And now the others were probably never going to talk to her again.

Waves of embarrassment rolled over her as she pedaled blindly, spurred on by the adrenaline of fear (she hated conflict) and her eagerness to right the afternoon's wrong. She prayed that the others would give her a second chance — that they'd just accept the fact that she'd made a horrible mistake, and couldn't they all just be friends again? She also cursed her new haircut, blaming it for getting her into this in the first place. If she hadn't waved at Sloan (something she never would've done with her old haircut); if she hadn't up and joined her on the beach (ditto); if . . . if . . . She wished she had her old hair back. This new cut was just getting her into trouble, making her think she was someone she was not. Or not yet, anyway.

⛵

Back at The Sound, Kate saw that Gee's car wasn't in the driveway and remembered Gee had her book club meeting tonight at her friend's house. Phew. Still, Kate raced into the kitchen. A pot of chili bubbled on the stove, but there was no one to be seen. *Guess they weren't too worried about me,* thought Kate, kind of surprised.

Now that she was home, and knew for sure that Sheila and Gee weren't pacing the front hall, calling the police department to track her down, Kate had to face the music. She dawdled a bit in the kitchen, debating whether or not to sneak a before-dinner snack of Doritos and a Coke (Hillary's advice was still fresh in her mind), and delaying the inevitable trip down the hill to the Dorm. Finally, she decided she'd do better to go down to them than have them come up and discover her — her apology would have more weight if she made the effort to seek them out — so she trudged, with heavy feet and an even heavier heart, to the back door and down the hill.

But as she ducked through the hedge's tunnel and opened the gate, she could hear the laughter coming from inside the little house. Hmm. It didn't sound like anyone in there was furious, or even worried. She threw open the door, and saw her cousins and . . . Lark? They were all sitting around the coffee table, laughing heartily, with a pile of benefit coupons and certificates right in the middle of them.

"Hi, guys!" said Kate sheepishly.

"Hey," said Hillary, without smiling.

Neeve flicked her eyes at Kate, and Phoebe didn't even look up.

"Hi, Kate," said Lark, the only one who didn't seem mad at her.

Kate paused. Despite her guilt, she was still taken aback by her cousins' cool greeting of her, and a little unnerved by their apparent replacement of her with Lark. Didn't they care at all that she'd been missing for hours? Or hadn't they noticed? Her apologies dried in her throat.

"I'm back!" she ventured again, in a voice more singsongy and confident than she felt.

"Great," said Neeve in a tone that indicated it was anything but.

"Where's your new best friend?" sneered Phoebe, unable to contain herself.

"What? You mean Sloan?"

"Yes, I mean *Sloan*." The way that Phoebe spat the name out in disgust suddenly infuriated Kate. Apologizing was now out of the question, and she found herself in the unique position of defending Sloan to the cousins.

"She went home, too. And for your information, she is not my new best friend. She just happens to be very cool, unlike some people, and I enjoy hanging out with her." Oops. Kate hadn't meant to be quite so forceful. Now she was really in trouble. She glanced at Hillary, whose hand had flown to her mouth in surprise at Kate's vehemence.

Now Phoebe came out with both guns blaring. "By 'some people' you are obviously referring to me, and potentially the others. I'm sorry we suddenly don't meet your criteria for coolness anymore, and equally sorry for you — in fact, I pity you — that you have this new obsession with cool. If you'd listened to even one thing that Gee said at dinner the other night, you'd realize that you are chasing something worthless, and you will only end up hurting yourself. So good luck with your new cool best friend. And just wait 'til you see where cool gets you!"

Kate didn't have a comeback to that, so she spun on her heel and climbed the ladder to the loft, silently enraged. *Thank goodness I didn't already apologize!* she thought angrily.

Lark had stayed for dinner, which further irritated Kate. It wasn't that she didn't like Lark. She was nice enough. But Kate was ashamed that Lark had witnessed her casual betrayal of the cousins for Sloan, and their fight afterward; and her shame made her mad at Lark. In addition, she was mad that the cousins had so quickly replaced her with Lark — inviting her to dinner without even checking to see if Kate minded first. And she did! Because with Lark there, Kate felt self-conscious, like an outsider; and also, she was sickened by the thought that the other girls may have been discussing her or her behavior with Lark while she was still at the beach. Ugh! That would be so disloyal!

At the table, Kate's annoyance with Lark mounted. Lark seemed so impressed by the cousins — so eager to please, so eager to hang out with them, it made Kate uncomfortable. *It's kind of pathetic, actually,* she thought. And then, with a shock, she put down her spoon. *I hope that's not how I seem to Sloan!* she thought in a panic. *Overeager. Ugh!* When Neeve had invited Lark to stay for dinner, Lark had almost not believed Neeve was serious — like such an invitation was too good to be true. And the way she'd shown her true feelings — her total and complete joy at being asked — was suddenly so uncool. It reminded Kate of, well . . . herself. And that was what was embarrassing.

Kate was silent during dinner, but without Gee there, no one noticed or made an effort to draw her out. Phoebe and Neeve were basically not speaking to her, and Hillary just made general conversation. After dinner, she grabbed a couple of cookbooks from Gee's shelf — including some vegetarian one from the 1970s — and returned to the Dorm while the others stayed up to play games in the main house for a while. It felt weird, and lonely, to have the Dorm all to herself. She didn't quite know what to do.

Her skin was killing her, so she went up to the bathroom to look in the mirror. Gross! She *did* look like a lobster, just as

Sloan had anticipated — all red, and shiny, and kind of puffy. Her stomach was the most fried of all, and it hurt. She vowed never to wear a bikini again, and gingerly peeled it off, momentarily shocked by the stark outline of her suit on her skin. The burn was only on her front side, which really made it look worse, since her arms and legs were only half-colored, and kind of mottled along the edges. Kate sighed and looked more closely in the mirror. Sure enough, there were tiny sun blisters forming across the bridge of her nose and on her chest. But underneath the burn there was a strange kind of orange color, just faint. Kate hoped the self-tanner didn't have an orange cast to it; it would look so fake if it did.

Kate climbed into her bed to flip through the cookbooks, and soon fell so soundly asleep that she didn't even awaken when the others went arrived for bed.

"Katie!" The voice was full of horror, and Kate sat bolt upright in bed, alarmed. Daylight streamed in the windows of the loft.

"What?!"

It was Neeve. "What did you *do* to yourself?"

Huh?

Kate was not used to being woken up like this. Usually she was the first one awake. "What? What is it?"

"You're orange! Well, and red, a little. But mostly orange! Did you do self-*tanner*?" Neeve was incredulous.

Kate looked down at her arms, and the backs of her hands.

Frantically, she flipped her hands over and examined her palms. Then her legs, after yanking back the covers. All this in three seconds, before she flung herself out of bed and ran to the mirror that hung on the wall at one end of the loft.

Oh dear! Oh double oh deary dear! Kate was orange. From head to toe. And not just solid orange, but streaky, blotchy, hideous orange. She closed her eyes and opened them again, willing this to be a bad dream. But no. And with various sunburned parts of her still glowing Rudolph-red (though not as brightly as last night, thank goodness), she looked terrible. Like she had a disease or something.

Her hand flew to her mouth in horror, and she spun to face Neeve, who had a wry smile on her face. "What do I do?"

"Well, what *did* you do? That's what we need to know first." Neeve was out-and-out laughing now, and Hillary and Phoebe had sat up in their beds. Kate glanced at them and saw her own hideousness reflected back at her in their alarmed expressions. She looked terrible.

"I put self-tanner on yesterday at the beach. Without reading the instructions!" she wailed.

Neeve tut-tutted. "It's probably too late. You over-applied, and you didn't exfoliate first. And you sat in the sun, which is a major no-no. . . ."

But Kate was already turning on the shower. She slammed the door to the tiny bathroom right in Neeve's face and stripped down. Oh, why had she done this! She should have read the instructions! Why had she let Sloan talk her out of it? Or into it? Her instincts — however predictable, however old lady-ish or uncool — would never have let this happen. And she'd just ignored them! Aargh!

When the water reached the right temperature, she hopped in and began scrubbing. But her sunburn and the tiny blisters hampered her, and anyway, the damage was done. The self-tanner wouldn't come off. After a few moments, she turned off the water in defeat and emerged dripping. But what now? There was no way she could go to clinic.

Returning to the bedroom, she began rummaging through the basket of toiletries on her dresser top. Could she bleach away the stains with some hydrogen peroxide? Nope. Could she use cover-up? At least on her face? Ugh. She'd look like a clown.

The others were watching her in silence, and Phoebe now had an amused smirk on her face. Kate wheeled around.

"I guess you think I got what I deserved, huh?" It came out calmer than she felt.

Phoebe shrugged. "Yes. Because I don't like you when you're not acting like yourself."

Kate's eyes welled up. She really couldn't stand conflict. "Why are you being so mean to me?" she wailed.

Unlike Kate, who wore her heart (and everything else) on her sleeve, Phoebe didn't usually show it if she'd been hurt. "And how do you think you've been behaving, Miss I'm Going to Ditch My Own Flesh and Blood for Our Enemy?"

Kate slumped onto the end of her bed and hung her head.

"I'm sorry. I know I shouldn't have done that yesterday. I'm such a loser."

"Oh for Lord's sake! Don't be such a defeatist!" accused Neeve. "If you're going to upgrade your friends, at least have some style about it! Don't come whinging back to us less than twenty-four hours later, after you've made a fool of yourself. Get it together, lass!" Neeve's Irish words came racing in as they usually did when she got excited.

Kate gave a hearty sniff and tried to sit up straight. Hillary crawled out of bed and came to circle her arm around Kate's shoulders, which made Kate want to cry even harder. How could she possibly reject Hillary in favor of Sloan? What was she thinking?

"Listen," Hillary addressed everyone. "Kate's a little mixed up right now, and I think we need to cut her some slack. She made a bad choice yesterday — actually, a few bad choices," Hillary laughed, holding Kate at arm's length to take in the orange streaks. Neeve and Phoebe giggled, and so did Kate now, through her tears. "So let's give her a do-over, okay?" Hillary always resorted to sports analogies when emotions were running high.

Neeve and Phoebe appeared to be thinking it over. "Maybe you should apologize," Hillary prodded Kate.

"I'm sorry, you guys," Kate repeated.

"But how are we to know you won't do it again?" Phoebe was stern.

"I just won't," promised Kate.

"Wait, are we talking about ditching us for Sloan or using self-tanner?" asked Neeve with a grin. And everyone laughed. They were friends again. For now.

"I think I'm just not meant to be tan," moaned Kate. "Either artificially or otherwise."

"Most Irish people aren't," said Neeve sympathetically.

"But it looks so good. And tan people are so . . . cool-looking."

"For now," said Hillary. "Just wait 'til later."

"When they're dead from skin cancer!" added Neeve ominously.

"True." Kate knew this. She'd just have to cross the tan thing off her list. It wasn't for her.

With the cousins on shakily good terms again, the real drama took center stage. "Now what am I going to do about all this orange?" begged Kate. "I can't go to clinic like this!"

"There's no way Gee will let you bag," said Hillary thoughtfully.

"Especially for reasons of vanity that are self-inflicted," added Phoebe.

"And it could be days before it fades," added Neeve.

"Aargh!" Kate collapsed back onto her bed.

"I think we can figure something out," said Phoebe, rising from her bed.

CHAPTER TWELVE

Yes!

$\mathcal{K}$ate felt like a celebrity hiding from the paparazzi. Phoebe had dredged up an oversized, long-sleeved t-shirt, long linen pants, a fishing hat with a wide brim that could be pulled down, and a thin layer of white zinc oxide for her face (she told Kate to pretend it was doctors' orders). Kate had balked at wearing gloves to clinic, so she let the sleeves of the t-shirt hang down over her hands. Where yesterday she'd been excited for people at clinic to notice her new look, today she dreaded the curious stares of her fellow sailors. So she just kept her hat pulled low and practiced ducking her chin to avoid eye contact. And she didn't plan a snack to bring.

At breakfast, Gee was shocked and then amused by her appearance, which gave Kate a taste of what lay in store for her in the day or two ahead. Most of all, she wanted to avoid Sloan, who was sure to want to chat after having spent the afternoon together yesterday.

But Kate couldn't have been more wrong. At clinic, Kate struggled not to raise her hand in greeting when she saw her new friend. She had to remind herself that Sloan would probably tease her and make her feel like a dork for her outfit or her spazzy self-tanner application. Yet when Sloan passed the cousins on her way out to the dock, she didn't even acknowledge them. She was focused on the new girl who had joined her group as a counselor in training, and she gave the Callahans a cool once-over without a hint of recognition as she passed. Even Kate had to admit that it was bizarre. She wasn't totally incognito in her outfit; wouldn't Sloan even realize who she was by association?

"Hi, Sloan," she'd murmured, half-wanting Sloan to say hi and half-not. But Sloan had breezed by without so much as a nod of her head.

The girls watched her pass; then Neeve said, "We got the look-through."

"The what?" Kate was mortified to distraction by Sloan's rebuff of her greeting.

"It's what the super-cool older girls at my school in Kenya used to do. They look through you like you're not even there. Even if you've spent the whole week all buddy-buddy with one of them, like, working on the yearbook, if she's with her friends and she sees you, she looks right through you. It's so lame."

Phoebe was surprised. "Are you, of all people, actually bothered by that?"

"Nah." Most social slights rolled off Neeve like water off a duck's back. "It's actually kind of funny, because it takes more energy to ignore someone who's saying hi to you than it does to just say hi back."

Kate mulled that one over. It was true. So maybe Sloan was so busy paying attention to ignoring Kate that she couldn't even say hi. Or something like that.

Then Lark joined the cousins. She was full of gratitude for the invitation of the previous night, and wanting to chat. The other three quickly fell into an animated conversation with her, and Kate felt alternately maddened by Lark's presumptuousness at just barging right into their group and also embarrassed by what Lark had witnessed the day before. Most of all, she felt left out.

And then, "I'm getting my ears pierced tomorrow," Kate blurted, interrupting.

Lark and the cousins stopped talking and stared at her, stunned partially by her uncharacteristic rudeness and partially by the news.

"I thought your parents wouldn't let you," said Neeve bluntly.

Kate was embarrassed at being portrayed as a baby in front of Lark. "Well, I haven't asked in ages. I'm sure it's okay now."

"You'll have to call them to check, though," said Hillary, not unkindly.

"Just as a formality," Kate said haughtily.

The others exchanged glances. "Where are you going to have it done?" asked Phoebe.

"Gullboutique," said Kate.

"Oh, that's where I had mine done! It's nice!" said Hillary. Kate flashed her a smile of gratitude for her enthusiasm.

"Gee will have to go with you," said Phoebe. "Since you're a minor."

"What?"

"You're underage. You'll need a grown-up to take you," said Phoebe.

"I don't know about that . . . ," said Kate.

"I do," said Phoebe firmly. "I had to."

"But that was in Florida," said Kate, losing her confidence.

"All I'm saying is, once your parents say yes, you'll have to have Gee speak to them, and then she can take you."

"Hmm." Kate didn't really like this proposal. She wasn't at all sure that her parents were ready to change their minds, especially so close to the real deadline. And she knew Gee wouldn't take her without her parents' explicit permission. *Oh, why did Phoebe always have to be such a know-it-all?* fumed Kate silently.

The topic was exhausted for now, since her plans would be on hold until she talked to her parents. The other three turned their attention back to Lark, and Kate let her eyes drift across the small knots of kids and counselors until her gaze settled on Sloan. She thought of Sloan's ear-piercing offer of the day before and shuddered at the idea. As if!

▲

After clinic, Kate convinced the other girls to bag going to town, pointing out that they'd done a lot of work already, and that she was orange, anyway, and couldn't really go out asking for donations. Instead, she talked them into doing a lemonade stand and donating the proceeds to the clinic.

"Okay, Kate," agreed Hillary finally. "But tomorrow, you're going to have to go back. We all will." Kate agreed and instantly pushed the thought out of her mind. When they arrived home, Kate whipped up a quick batch of Toll House cookies, while the others squeezed endless lemons, and at the end they'd raised $44 at the bottom of Gee's driveway in only two hours. (Halfway through, Phoebe announced that she was sure that once they'd left the house, Gee had dialed up all of her friends and asked them to swing by; the clientele was suspiciously familiar and had arrived in nearly alphabetical order, as if Gee had just worked her way through her phone book!)

That night, Gee took them to play miniature golf at an old-fashioned-style course that had recently reopened on the waterfront near Hagan's Marina. The girls spent ages getting dressed, since they figured there might be boys there, and there was a lot of clothes-borrowing and makeup application going on in the Dorm before they left. Maybe it was Kate's imagination, but the others had seemed to be talking more than ever about earrings and which ones to wear. Phoebe tried on a pair of Neeve's, but decided they were too tribal-looking (even for her, the hippie!), and instead wore a pair of Hillary's studs. Neeve wore a pair of Phoebe's mid-length danglies, and Hillary wore hoops with charms that looked really cute, because she'd pulled her long, strawberry-blond curls up into a twist, exposing her pretty neck. Kate, of course, had no sassy earrings to lend or borrow. And she had to wear a long skirt and a long-sleeved cotton turtleneck sweater to hide her orange-ness. She put on a baseball cap and pulled the visor low over her face. This orange stuff was getting old.

Gee complimented their "lovely accessories" and made them all go back and wash off at least half of their makeup. Then they piled into Gee's ancient Volvo, and that was where Kate had her brainstorm. Why couldn't she just ask Gee to take her for the ear piercing, and never even ask her parents? It was no biggie. Just a new way of accessorizing. Gee would say yes for sure. Kate relaxed back into her seat and leaned her head against the Volvo's totally uncomfortable headrest. There. That was one thing solved. They could go tomorrow. She'd just have to phrase it properly so that Gee would know it wasn't a big deal.

Mini-golf was fun. Each girl picked a different colored ball, and they shrieked and laughed as they played their way around the little course. Phoebe turned out to be the best, carefully lining up her shot through the windmill, under the chicken coop, into the lighthouse. Since it was only five-thirty, there weren't that many people there at first, but as they played, it started to fill up. There were teenagers to watch, and cute boys, and funny little kids who swung their clubs enthusiastically in big arcs, sending balls careening across the course.

Despite the excellent people-watching, by the eighteenth

hole, Kate was bursting. She had to ask Gee about her ears or she'd die from holding it in. Phoebe, Neeve, and Hillary decided to go ask the counter person about a donation, and Kate was thankfully excused because she was orange. Kate bent over to line up her putt into the volcano, and chose that moment to speak up, so she wouldn't have to look Gee right in the eye.

"Hey, Gee?"

"Yes, dear?" Gee was distracted. She'd missed the hole on her first try and the others had generously insisted that she try again. She was watching Kate to see how she played it, and then she'd go again.

"I was wondering . . ." Tick. She hit the ball and missed the tunnel. The ball bounced off the side of the volcano with a hollow *thunk*. Kate stepped aside so Gee could place her ball on the tee.

"Are you busy tomorrow afternoon?" She was stalling and she knew it. She held her breath.

"Umm." Gee hit the ball and looked up. "No, sweetheart. I don't think there's anything that can't wait. What did you have in mind?" The ball rolled wide, and Gee rolled her eyes in frustration.

"Oh." Kate moved in to hit her ball again. "I was thinking I should, uh . . ." She hit the ball, and it went through the tunnel in the volcano.

"Great shot, Katie!" Gee was genuinely pleased, and stepped in to hit.

Kate screwed up all of her courage and tried to keep her

voice light. "I was thinking I'd like to go, just, get my ears pierced. I think I'm ready."

"Oh!" Gee hit her ball through and pumped her fist in the air in a very uncharacteristic gesture. "Yes!"

Kate's heart leaped. "Yes?"

"Sorry, dear. I meant the ball. Oh, getting your ears pierced. Why would you want to do that? Your ears are lovely just as they are."

Kate's heart sank. "Thanks. But, you know. Everyone has them. And it would be so fun to be able to, ah, wear the bead earrings I've been making with the cousins, and, you know, share earrings with them. Stuff like that." She averted her eyes.

"My generation didn't believe in ear piercing. It was considered cheap-looking, or even barbaric. See?" Gee unclipped an earring to show that she'd never pierced hers, which Kate already knew.

"Yeah, but it's really in now. And, sorry, but times have changed." Kate was trying not to let desperation creep into her voice.

Gee looked at her carefully. "What does your mom think about pierced ears?"

Darn! Kate couldn't lie, so she'd have to choose her words carefully. "Well, we haven't talked about it lately." That was true. But what else could she add to make Gee say yes?

There was a pause, and then Gee said. "I'm not crazy about pierced ears myself, but if your mother thinks it's okay, then I'm happy to take you."

Yay! "Thanks, Gee!"

". . . So just call her when we get home tonight and I'll talk to her and get her okay." She patted Kate on the head and went to get her ball.

Aargh! Kate followed Gee around the volcano through a cloud of steam.

The cousins came running back, waving a coupon for a round of mini-golf for eight people, so Gee and Kate stopped to ooh and aah over their success. Then they stood at the end of the hole to wait for Kate and Gee to finish, and while they stood they watched a group of teenage boys playing behind them. Kate glanced at the boys — one of them looked familiar, but she couldn't place him. As she stole another glance at him, Sloan joined his group.

Phoebe gave a quiet whistle. "Look at your best friend now," she said to Kate in whisper. Sloan was wearing the world's tiniest miniskirt and a halter top, plus gobs of makeup. No one was surprised that she didn't say hi. She was obviously pretending not to know them, and they weren't about to approach her.

"She's not my best friend, Phoebe!" Kate was getting tired of the whole Sloan thing, and she wished more than ever that she'd never gone to sit with her yesterday on the beach.

"Those guys are super-cute." Hillary studied them through narrowed eyes. "Why are they hanging out with a jerk like her?"

Neeve slugged her in the arm. "Don't be so clueless, Hill! The girls who are the meanest to other girls are always the ones the guys go for. It's just a law of life."

"Boys are so annoying," sighed Phoebe wistfully. Her tone of voice indicated that they were anything but.

"I agree," sighed Gee, resting her head on Phoebe's shoulder. She'd come up behind them, and they hadn't noticed.

"Gee!" protested Phoebe. Everyone laughed.

"Come on, girls. Let's finish up here, then head over to Coolidge's for a nice dinner. Don't let the boys know you're interested; that's the way to get their attention for sure. The girls who fawn all over them get their attention at first, but it's the mysterious ones who keep it."

Coolidge's! That's where Kate had seen him before. But wait! Wasn't that where Sloan had said the cute older boys worked? The ones she was waiting for that day on the beach? So maybe she hadn't been lying! Kate looked at Sloan and felt a mixture of admiration, jealousy, and also relief. Jealousy because she wished she were brave enough to be over there, hanging out with them and laughing, playfully stealing the cute boy's ball so he would chase her, the way Sloan was now. Admiration because Sloan was obviously good at flirting, and Kate was not. And relief, because she was glad Sloan wasn't a total liar, and also because she didn't have to be over there herself, thinking of funny things to say and do with the boys. Leave that to Sloan.

She turned to follow the others, but took one more backward look. Surprisingly, she felt suddenly sorry for Sloan, trying so hard, and as she started to turn away, Sloan caught her eye. Kate smiled, but Sloan didn't smile back. Instead, her eyes looked beseechingly at Kate as if to say, "Help! Don't leave me here alone! Please be my friend!"

Kate was shocked by the look, and turned quickly back to the cousins to compose herself for a second. But when she turned back to Sloan, Sloan had turned away, and Kate wondered if she'd just misinterpreted Sloan's look. *Weird,* she thought. *But why would Sloan wish I was staying with her?*

Thursday was overcast, with a heavy dull grayness hanging overhead — clouds so low Kate felt she could almost touch them. Clinic had been canceled due to a storm warning, and the girls were free for the morning. Kate normally would've been elated by this turn of events, but today it only meant one thing: they were now free to go to town for donations in the morning. Kate's orangeness wasn't even a decent excuse for her anymore; she had faded to a pale peach and no longer looked weird to strangers. So with a churning stomach and feet of lead, she and the others biked into Eastport Harbor after a late breakfast. Town was busy with vacationers and day-trippers who'd come over on the ferry to enjoy Gull's beautiful Macaroni Beach, but had been kept in town shopping by the iffy weather. To Kate, that meant that she'd be likely to have an audience in the stores on her list. It couldn't have been worse.

Kate had tried suggesting they go out in teams of two, but the others cautioned her that she'd already missed a few days due to ditching them, and then orangeness, and now they were way behind. So she'd reluctantly parked her bike on Market Street with the cousins, and watched them go off, bravely and happily. She was jealous of their confidence, and felt lonely in knowing that the task ahead was much more daunting for her than it was for anyone else. Slowly, she backtracked to Broad Street to check in at the Old Mill, where at least she'd already done some legwork.

While she walked, she prayed that the owner wouldn't be there. She didn't even care if the woman hadn't left her anything — if she hadn't even received Kate's note. She just couldn't bear to be subjected to the pitying kindness she'd received at the fabric store, if she was to discover that the Old Mill had already made its donation to Sloan.

Outside, she hesitated, trying to peer into the high windows of the mill. Finally, she gave up and went in slowly, as if she were walking to her own execution: forlorn and slumped. But her guardian angel must have been watching over her that day, for when she'd reached the counter and stammered out enough words to form a coherent explanation of why she was there, the salesgirl (a different one this time) ducked her head below the counter and pulled out an envelope marked "Kate Callahan." Inside was a coupon for an easel and a set of oil paints and brushes, donated by the owner in response to the note Kate had left. Triumph!

Kate bounced out of the store, clutching her envelope and practically kissing it in her joy and relief. That had been so easy!

Blindly, she walked a few hundred feet up Broad Street to the corner, and then collapsed in relief onto a bench on the sidewalk. *Maybe I could just write notes to everyone!* she thought, staring at the shoppers all around her on the street, bustling confidently from store to store. *Would that work?* She scratched a bug bite while she considered it, then absentmindedly pulled an alcohol swab from her tote bag to cool the itch.

While she stood, ministering to her bug bite, Sloan Bicket emerged from the wide front door of the stately white-columned Coolidge House across the street. Kate dropped the swab back into her bag, suddenly self-conscious about her preparedness. She looked around; there was nowhere to hide.

Sloan saw her instantly, and a smile lit up her face. "Kate!" she called, waving. Kate was taken aback by her friendliness and fought the urge to look over her shoulder for another Kate, hiding behind her, who might be worthy of Sloan's attention.

"Hi, Sloan." Kate was tentative. She was suspicious of Sloan, and dreaded getting involved with Sloan again, lest she anger her cousins. But Sloan's strange look from mini-golf the night before had stayed with her, and Kate felt unsure of her usual feelings for Sloan. Although her brain was telling her to move on, her heart kept her rooted to the spot. Anyway, Sloan was already crossing the street to talk to her.

"What brings you into town this morning? Shopping for souvenirs?"

Kate's sympathy was quickly squashed by annoyance. Sloan loved to imply that the Callahans were tourists, and it drove them crazy. Kate answered flatly, "No, Sloan. What brings you in?"

"Donations, of course." She swung a small beach bag that was filled with envelopes, menus, fliers, and other paperwork, and opened it with a flourish for Kate's inspection. Kate peered inside.

"Huh," was all she could manage. Sloan looked at her in disbelief.

"Aren't you impressed? I've gotten some of the best donations that have ever been given in the history of this event. I got free sailing lessons and a boat charter from the Hagans, eight private sessions with a physical trainer, a house appraisal from the real estate company, a catered dinner at home from Coolidge House, a hot air balloon ride on the mainland, a year's supply of meat from the Bicket Bouquet . . ."

Kate's eyes had started to glaze over during Sloan's speech. She couldn't believe all the amazing stuff Sloan had secured. Her easel and paints seemed paltry by comparison. But suddenly, like a bolt of lightning, a thought struck her: *This little competition matters more to Sloan than to me, or anyone, actually.* And then another tiny thought — a wisp of a thought, really — occurred to her, too: *Maybe Sloan keeps it going because it gives her something to talk to us about!* But no. That was impossible. *Sloan has plenty of other things to do, doesn't she?*

Kate suddenly realized that Sloan was looking at her expectantly, awaiting a reaction to her amazing list. She didn't know *what* to say, so what she said was: "Wow. I'm going to get my ears pierced . . . right now, actually." There. She'd just decided. Because it was something she was terrified to do, it would make her feel better about herself if she could accomplish at least that today.

"Where?" asked Sloan, nonplussed by the news.

"At Gullboutique." Actually, it was one of the places on Kate's list. Maybe she could write a note while she was there?

"Oh, I'll go with you. Then I can ask them for a donation," said Sloan.

"Fine," said Kate. "Come along." She didn't really care; her newfound competitiveness had faded, replaced by her usual anxiety. Anyway, now she'd be able to tell the cousins that Sloan had gotten the donation from Gullboutique before she did. What did it matter anyway, who got the donation? Wasn't the point just to get it?

The two walked side by side down Market Street, then crossed to make their way to Gullboutique. As they crossed, Kate caught sight of Hillary and Neeve up the street walking toward them, and she quickly looked away; she didn't want them to know she'd seen them. *Aha! So they'd teamed up! That wasn't fair!* Then, out of the corner of her eye, Kate could tell they'd noticed her. *Oh dear*, she thought. *Here we go again.* The two stopped to stare, but Kate didn't look again, choosing to keep them in her peripheral vision. But she could feel their stares like daggers in her back as she and Sloan proceeded into the store. *Well tough*, she decided suddenly. *Maybe I'll team up with Sloan and see how they like that!*

Inside Gullboutique, there were a few small racks of super-trendy clothes, more for grown-ups than kids, plus cases of jewelry, sunglasses, fake tattoos and stick-on jewels, and hair accessories. On top of the cases were sumptuous piles of folded scarves and beach sarongs, and stacks of squishy sweaters. One wall held shoe boxes of cute flip-flops and strappy sandals, with higher shelves groaning with purses and swanky beach bags. A small sign on the counter said FREE EAR PIERCING WITH PURCHASE OF STUDS! and there was an easel with a black velvet—covered board on it that held dozens of pairs of small gold earrings.

Kate immediately drew up to the counter and began gazing at her choices. Small gold balls? Seashells like Sloan's? Little gold sailor's knots? None of them were cheap, but the price included the piercing, so she could rationalize the expense. After all, pierced ears were so cool they were practically price-less: she wouldn't have been surprised if they'd charged $100! The decision making distracted her for a moment, until she settled on a pair of medium-sized gold balls for $58. And then her nervousness moved in again, this time in the form of a flutter in her empty stomach. She looked around for a salesgirl, to get someone to help her, and one of them looked up from across the room, smiled, and came to speak to Kate.

"Hi," she said, tossing her long honey-blond ponytail over one shoulder. She was wearing a halter, sarong, and flip-flops, and she smelled like coconut. She reminded Kate of the summer babysitters she'd had growing up. "Can I help you?"

"Hi." Kate smiled nervously. "Um, yes, I'd like to buy these earrings, right here please?" She pointed to the balls.

"Okay, sweetie." The girl bent to unfasten them from the board, and Kate waited until the girl had her back to her and couldn't see her face. Then she said, "And I'll need the piercing, too, please."

The girl turned with a smile to look at Kate. "Oh! You don't have your ears pierced yet! That's so cute!"

Kate blushed and fingered one of her naked earlobes. "Yeah. . . ."

The girl assessed Kate's face for a minute. "They're going to look great. You have terrific bone structure in your face."

Kate was pleased. Good bones. Just like those houses on the remodeling shows! Ha!

"Okay. Well, let me just tell the manager, and she'll get the gun."

Kate's smile faded quickly. The gun?! Kate had heard it was painful, but a gun? What did they do, shoot you through the ear? Oh dear. This was going to be even worse than she'd thought. She looked around for Sloan, but Sloan was, of course, engrossed in conversation with the manager, no doubt securing the donation of an entirely new wardrobe for the lucky winner at the benefit. The salesgirl waited politely for a break in their conversation before she could ask for the gun. (The gun!)

Meanwhile, Kate tried to distract herself by thinking about what she would say to the cousins when she met them at Callie's Cupboard for lunch in an hour. How could she explain why she'd been walking with Sloan? And what would she say about the donations she'd not yet gotten? Well, she'd just have to distract *them* with the exciting news about her pierced ears!

She could see the salesgirl coming back to her now, and her stomach lurched in dread at the pain that was coming, too. But instead, the girl said, "Sweetie, is your mom meeting you here?"

Huh? "No, my mom's in New York. . . ." Kate was confused. Sloan came over just then, waving her envelope triumphantly in the air. "A rainbow of pashminas, one for every outfit!" she crowed. "Isn't that great?"

But Kate was too preoccupied to answer. She was still looking at the salesgirl in bewilderment. Why did the girl care where her mom was?

". . . Gee, that's too bad. See, we need a parent or guardian's permission to pierce your ears if you're under eighteen. And I'm guessing you're about . . . thirteen or fourteen?" She smiled in a friendly manner.

Unfortunately for the salesgirl, this was just the straw that broke the camel's back. Kate was devasted. First of all, because Phoebe had been right that Kate would need an adult's permission to get her ears pierced. Second of all, because she wouldn't be showing up to meet the others with pierced ears, which would've made a success of the morning. Thirdly, because Sloan had just waltzed in and gotten the donation that, truth be told, Kate should've just tried to get herself. And finally, because she was so frustrated with herself for the scaredy-cat way she'd been acting lately. But instead of being sad, Kate got mad. Really mad. Like, red rage mad. Like the other day, at White's.

"Fine," she snapped at the salesgirl, who looked bewildered by Kate's sudden change of mood. "Then never mind." And Kate turned on her heel and stormed out of the store.

Blindly, she rushed up Market Street, past the police and fire departments (which usually intimidated her so much that she had to cross the street, but today she took no notice of them), past the town park, and over to the grassy area surrounding the Lost at Sea monument. There, she finally calmed down enough to gather her wits and assess the situation. She was a loser: she was scared to try anything, and even when she did finally try something scary, it never worked out. She either turned orange, or got turned down, or got turned away, and she was sick of it. Absentmindedly, she read the names of the sailors lost at sea that were inscribed on the boat-shaped monument and thought about the horror they must've felt as they died horrible deaths out in the ocean, far from home and comfort. She shuddered.

Ear piercing didn't even come close. And then she heard someone calling her name. It was Sloan again.

She turned slowly around to see Sloan sauntering across Fisher's Path. Sloan hadn't chased her — she was hardly the type to run after someone — but the fact that she had come after Kate at all was surprising. Kate's blood was still boiling, but she was intrigued.

When Sloan reached her, she said in her usual snotty drawl, "That was so lame. I couldn't believe that they wouldn't do your ears for you."

"Yeah." Kate's voice was clipped and short.

There was a pause. "Like I said the other day, I could do them for you."

"Ha!" Kate laughed a mirthless laugh. As if.

"No, really. I've done it lots of times." Sloan looked away, then looked back at Kate. Kate's stare was penetrating. She knew Sloan was lying and she was tempted this time to call her on it, but instead Sloan withered under Kate's gaze, which could've melted metal. "Okay, twice. I've done it twice." Kate felt a surge of power. She'd just made Sloan correct herself in a lie! And it had been easy! All she had to do was be strong and silent and . . . mad.

Suddenly she thought, *What the heck? Why not let Sloan do my ears? That would be an even braver thing to do than get them pierced professionally.*

"Okay," agreed Kate.

"Okay?" repeated Sloan in wonderment. And then, "O-*kay*. So let's go."

In silence, Kate followed Sloan to her house, which was two blocks from town. As they ambled down the bumpy brick sidewalk underneath a canopy of trees rustling in the cool, damp breeze blowing in from the Atlantic, Kate refused to allow herself to think about what she was going to do. Instead, she pulled a pink cotton cardigan from her tote bag and paused to pull it on. Sloan waited in companionable silence until Kate was ready to continue.

They soon reached the Bickets' gray saltbox. It rose up from nearly the edge of the sidewalk, with a flat, unadorned front side that gave away nothing about its residents, other than that they were obsessively tidy. The front of the house was excruciatingly neat, with flawlessly painted white trim, a white picket fence in perfect repair, and low hedges around the foundation that looked as if they'd been trimmed by someone using a level and a ruler. Sloan opened the front door and called, "Anybody home?" But no one replied, and she shut the door and crossed the flagstone floor of the dim front hall to climb the stairs to her room. Kate followed. Having been there before, she knew where she was going and had little need to examine the Bickets' stark antique furniture and general lack of coziness. However, she needed something to distract herself from the coming event, so she counted the steep bare stairs. One, two, three . . .

Up in Sloan's room, Sloan assembled the tools of her trade like a coroner getting ready for an autopsy. Alcohol, cotton balls, a match, a needle, a pen, and some plain gold studs.

As she arranged things, she talked, nearly to herself, because Kate was now sitting on the edge of her bed like a zombie, in a state of suspended animation. She couldn't believe what she was about to do, and yet it seemed inevitable. Of course Sloan Bicket should be allowed to pierce her ears. Of course.

"Okay, so what I'm going to do is . . . first, I mark your ears." Sloan took the pen and solemnly approached Kate. She drew a tiny blue dot on each ear, checking back and forth to make sure they lined up. Kate gazed at Sloan's ears from up close. The earrings looked so safe just nestled there in her lobes. It was hard to believe that there'd been any pain involved in getting them there. Doubt began to creep in then, but Kate quickly reminded herself that zillions of people all over the world had pierced ears, so how badly could it really hurt? She looked in the mirror that Sloan offered her and nodded mutely to let Sloan know the marks looked okay. Then she fought the urge to suck her thumb.

"Now I sterilize the needle. . . ." Sloan pushed her tongue between her lips in concentration as she held the needle over a lit match until it blackened in the flame. Then she blew out the match, shook the needle to cool it, and swabbed it with some alcohol. "Okay. Now . . ." She crossed the room to where Kate sat and Kate stiffened, bracing herself for the pain.

Sloan stuck her tongue out again, and steadied her hand against Kate's cheek. Then she began to push. And strangely enough, it didn't hurt as badly as Kate would've thought. But the way she could hear the layers of skin popping as Sloan strained to push the needle through, well, that was actually really gross. Disgusting. Tears leaked out of the corners of Kate's eyes, and Sloan graciously pretended not to notice, which was very unlike her. Or perhaps she really didn't notice, so hard was she concentrating on her task.

"There!" The last layer was punctured and the needle was now sticking directly though Kate's ear.

"Don't look!" ordered Sloan. I'm just getting the earring and I'm going to push it through the hole now."

Kate nodded mutely. Her anger had nearly run its course, and its dulling effects had all but worn off. Fear was rushing into the void it had left, and queasiness, too. She had to look. Across the room was a mirror, and in a flash, Kate was there, peering at the needle jammed through her ear, and the tiny trickle of warm blood that she was just beginning to feel as it made its descent down her neck.

Oh dear.

Kate sat down heavily on the floor. The sight of blood had always made her faint — she even had to close her eyes, lie down, and wear an iPod when she got blood drawn at the doctor's office, or she'd pass out.

Sloan turned in alarm. "Are you alright?"

"I'm just . . . I think I need to . . ." Kate put her head between her knees, but it didn't do much, since she was sitting on the floor.

"Don't get blood on the rug or my mom will kill me. She'll kill me if she finds out I did this." Sloan was truly afraid, and this was something new. The novelty of someone as cool as Sloan actually being scared of someone was almost enough to perk Kate up.

"Can I get you some juice or something?" asked Sloan.

"Uh, sure."

"Okay. I'll be right back." Sloan started out the door and then turned back, her hand palm-out in midair. "Just don't faint, alright?"

Kate nodded, and stuck her thumb in her mouth. Just for a minute, she rationalized. It's an emergency.

After she drank the juice in silence, she and Sloan decided that perhaps it wasn't such a good idea if they continued the process. The good thing was that it was Sloan who really talked Kate out of it. And the more Kate realized that Sloan didn't want to continue, the stronger Kate could be about wanting to continue, which made her look good. In fact, as they cleaned up the mess, put tiny Band-Aid spots on either side of Kate's ear, and walked to meet the others at Callie's Cupboard, Kate began to think that *not* getting her ears pierced was one of the bravest things she'd ever done.

Kate felt a new intimacy and comfort with Sloan, now that they were practically blood sisters. She didn't even need to summon up her courage to talk to Sloan, as she usually did, but instead found herself having a conversation with Sloan that was so natural she wouldn't have ever thought it possible.

"Why do you care about the clinic benefit so much?" she asked.

Sloan was quiet for a moment. "Because my mom works there."

Huh! That was a surprise. "What does she do?"

"Spends time away from me and my brother," Sloan said angrily, tacking on a fake laugh at the end to soften the harshness of her words.

"No, really." Kate felt bad for her.

"She's a nurse practitioner and a researcher. She works for the, like, general doctor there."

"Oh." Kate hadn't known that. She'd just assumed Mrs. Bicket worked at the Bicket Bouquet with the rest of the family. "And that's why you want to get so many donations for the clinic? Because she works there?" Kate hadn't forgotten her earlier revelation, but now, as Phoebe would say, the plot was thickening.

"Well, I thought maybe it'd be a good way to get her to notice me," said Sloan in a small voice. Kate didn't know what to say, so she made a little joke out of fit.

"I'm sure she notices you! You're living in the same house! You probably run into each other in the bathroom sometimes!"

Sloan gave another little forced laugh, but she seemed relieved that Kate was trying to defuse the intensity of the conversation.

"Yeah! And in the kitchen, on holidays!" Kate laughed, too, this time, but she felt bad that she wasn't following through on the honesty that Sloan had offered her. It was just too much to take in: The Confessions of Sloan Bicket. Why would Sloan want to tell her this stuff anyway? Sure, Kate's friends back home came to her with all of their problems, but Sloan was way cooler than Kate. So why would she need Kate's advice or approval?

Instantly, with Kate's joking, the closeness they'd felt when they'd begun the walk evaporated, and Kate felt guilty. She shouldn't have done that. She should've let Sloan talk. The gray of the day had blown inland while they were at Sloan's — the storm had never materialized, and a blue sky was peeking out of the bumpy white clouds overhead. Kate tried to think of something to say to recapture the mood of sharing that she'd just wrecked.

"Oh, good," said Sloan, interrupting Kate's thoughts. "Sun."

"Yuck," said Kate, giving the sky a dirty look. "I prefer rainy days. And I especially hate it when a day starts out all cozy and

rainy and then turns sunny. Then you're expected to go outside and accomplish something. It's such a bummer."

Sloan looked at her askance. "Most people prefer being
outdoors, in nice weather. Ask anyone."

"Not me," said Kate with a vehement shake of her head.
"All of my favorite things to do are inside: cooking,
uh . . ." — she glanced at Sloan and decided to tell the truth,
as Sloan had, just moments ago — ". . . knitting, needlepoint, decorating, painting. . . . The only good thing about
outdoors is flowers. And anyway, you can have them inside
once they're grown." Kate laughed. "You can even grow them
inside, if you have a greenhouse!"

"Weird," said Sloan, eyeing Kate as if she were some sort of
freak.

But Kate didn't really mind. She was almost offering herself up for Sloan to harsh on, to allow Sloan to regain her
usual composure. She already knew where Sloan stood on the
subject of knitting, anyway. They chatted aimlessly as they
continued their walk, Kate purposely avoiding sensitive top-
ics, and Sloan seeming to do the same.

It was nearly one o'clock by the time they reached Callie's
Cupboard, and the others were so frantic with worry by the
time Kate and Sloan arrived that they forgot to show how
much they hated Sloan. Instead they sort of acted like she
wasn't there, because they were so concerned with where Kate
had been.

Kate began waving off their concerns in a casual way that was very Sloan-like, and then Hillary noticed her ear.

"Hey! What happened to your ear?"

"Oh, no biggie," said Kate with an uncharacteristic swagger in her voice. She was feeling pretty proud of herself after her experience with Sloan, fainting or no fainting.

But Sloan, to whom Kate would be forever grateful for this moment, no matter what evil things she did, spoke up. "Oh my God, you should've seen it! She wanted me to pierce her ears, and there was blood everywhere and a needle sticking out, and I wanted to stop, but she wouldn't let me. . . ." And on and on she went. Kate didn't mind that Sloan was squarely placing all of the blame on her; it just made Kate sound cooler. And a warm feeling of happiness bloomed in her chest when she saw the cousins looking at her incredulously.

"Who are you? And what have you done with our Kate?" demanded Neeve with a smile as she pulled Kate in for a hug. "Our Kate would never do any of that stuff! She's a scaredy-cat!"

Kate grinned over Neeve's shoulder. "You're right. She's too much of a chicken."

Phoebe huffed. "Absolutely ridiculous. You could get gangrene. Or worse. I can't believe you did that!" But Kate could tell she was a little impressed.

"You're one tough cookie," said Hillary appraisingly. "I knew you had it in you!"

Kate glanced at Sloan to flash her a smile of thanks, and

what she saw surprised her. Sloan's eyes were sad, and there was a small rueful smile on her lips as she watched the scene of the cousins all together. It was clearer than ever now that Sloan was envious! Of them! And she was supposed to be the cool one!

Sloan felt Kate's eyes on her, and she looked over, quickly re-arranging her features into her usual look of snotty boredom.

"Well, I've got things to do," she announced. No one really took notice; they were so busy discussing their own ear piercing experiences at that point. But Kate smiled at her.

"Thanks," she mouthed at Sloan. Sloan waved her off and began to walk out of Callie's. But then she turned back and came to Kate's side, reaching into her bag as she walked. She withdrew the envelope from Gullboutique and pressed it into Kate's hand, without anyone else noticing. "Here. This is yours," she said.

"Oh, I couldn't . . . ," Kate protested.

"Just take it," ordered Sloan. The old Sloan was back, and Kate gulped as fear reared its ugly head inside her once more. Sloan was still commanding and cool, and their shared moment of friendship would soon be a distant memory, one that Kate would sometimes doubt had ever happened.

CHAPTER FOURTEEN

Miss Munsfield

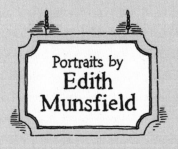

Portraits by
**Edith
Munsfield**

At lunch, the cousins wanted to hear every living detail of Kate's ear-piercing story, and she hammed it up, embellishing the story and making it much more gruesome than it actually had been. Wrap sandwiches were the specialty at Callie's, and Kate's turkey-and-cheese wrap kept unraveling as she gestured theatrically during her monologue. The other girls were in stitches as Kate described her own reaction to the piercing — she knew there was no point in continuing Sloan's generous lie that she'd been brave; she'd had to tell them she'd nearly fainted again, just from the sight of her own blood. Her wide-eyed delivery of the gory details and her exaggeration of the dangers were typical Kate, but for the first time in a while, she wasn't self-conscious about her role as chicken. It was funny, and comfortable, and — because she'd just done something so brave — it wasn't true. She wasn't a chicken right now, and it felt good. So she hammed it up for the others and didn't mind them laughing at her.

But for all of her honesty, she didn't tell them anything about how she'd felt close to Sloan; she didn't want to open that "new best friend" can of worms again. And she certainly didn't tell them how Sloan had seemed so lonely, and rejected. She'd never tell them that. Whether Sloan was her friend or not (she still couldn't tell), it just wouldn't be right to turn Sloan's deepest secrets into gossip. Most of all, she wouldn't tell them about Sloan's need to get donations to impress her mother, and how it made Kate feel bad — like they should drop out altogether and just let her finish it up. There was just no way to explain it without it sounding self-serving, and without it being mean to Sloan.

"So wait, did you get a donation from Gullboutique after all?" asked Neeve with a look of confusion on her face. Kate had kind of glossed over that portion of the story.

"Well . . ." Sloan had said it was hers. But she really couldn't lie to the others. "No. Sloan did. But she gave it to me to, ah, turn in." Kate snuck a look at Phoebe, nervous that Phoebe would accuse her of being Sloan's new best friend. The ear piercing event could look like an act of desperation on Kate's part, but sharing donations would really make her look guilty. Phoebe raised one eyebrow in that mature way of hers but said nothing, and Kate let out a breath in relief and looked away.

"But I did get a donation at the Old Mill!" cried Kate, suddenly remembering. She dove into her packed but well-organized tote bag and pulled out the envelope, waving it triumphantly.

"Yay!" cheered Hillary, and the others clapped for her. "Great job!" added Neeve.

"Yeah, so, I was thinking. . . . Maybe I'll just leave notes everywhere, and then, like, go back to see if anyone wants to donate." Kate gulped. She hoped the others would think this was a good idea, even though she knew very well that it really was a chicken thing to do. But if they approved, she'd definitely take that route.

Naturally, they didn't. "That's kind of a hassle, if you ask me," said Hillary.

"And why would you leave a note if the owner is right there?" asked Neeve, her eyes narrowed in confusion.

"Well, you know, so I don't put them on the spot. This way I give them time to think it through," Kate offered lamely, suspecting that she was beat.

Phoebe delivered the final blow, although her delivery was gentle. "But Kate, we don't have much time left, and that sounds really time-consuming, don't you think?"

Kate sighed. "I guess. It's just that I'm so bad at this. And I really hate it."

Hillary wiped her hands on her napkin, leaving green guacamole marks all over it. Kate fought the urge to reach across the table like a mother and wipe the streak of guacamole from Hillary's cheek. She held her breath until Hillary caught it with the napkin herself, and then crumpled the napkin onto her plate. Hillary then pushed the plate away and announced, "After lunch, you're coming with me."

Everyone turned to look at her.

"I am?" asked Kate.

"Yup," said Hillary firmly. And no one questioned her.

After Callie's, Hillary and Kate left the others, crossing Market Street and wandering slowly up to the corner. The florist shop all the way at the end of Broad Street was the next stop on Kate's list, and Hillary was going to help her with the donation process — they'd do it as a team. Hillary would do the asking and Kate would watch; no pressure. Kate was happy; this was what she'd wanted all along. And she was looking forward to the florist's shop, because she did love flowers. Sun or no sun, this day had certainly taken a turn for the better, and Kate was practically skipping as they walked.

"So, Hills, I don't mean to sound self-centered, but can we talk about the New Me for a minute? What else I should do?" Kate asked. She looked sideways at Hillary to see if she could read any annoyance on Hillary's face, but Hillary was her usual placid self.

"Well, the getting-in-shape part. I mean, you could exercise more."

Kate made a face.

Hillary laughed. "I guess you are fairly active. I mean, you ride your bike every day. So really, it's just about feeding your body better, like I said at the beach."

Kate nodded. The cookbooks she'd borrowed from Gee's kitchen were actually kind of appealing. She'd talked to Sheila a bit, and started a new journal for healthy recipes, even. Maybe she could make it fun. "Yeah, I think I can do that." She paused, and then she said fervently, "I can't give up chocolate, though! I'd rather die!"

Hillary laughed again. "You don't have to. Anyway, dark chocolate is actually good for you. Antioxidants and all that, and low fat, low sugar."

"Huh." Kate was surprised. Dark chocolate didn't taste bad enough to be healthy. She'd have to look into it.

Hillary continued, "So, braver, then?"

"Yeah." Kate glanced at the exercise gear in the window of Booker's and looked away, disinterested. But Hillary paused to examine some new running shoes. Kate waited patiently; she wasn't in a hurry to go asking for donations anyway.

"Right. But" — Hillary tore her eyes away from the window to look at Kate, and a look of confusion crossed her face — "braver, how? Like frogs and stuff, or adventures?"

"Hmm. Both?" They continued walking.

"Okay. So, if you want, I could catch a frog later, at home, and you could, like, hold it for a while."

Kate stopped in her tracks. "No way! Disgusting. And I'd probably get warts or something."

"O-kayyy . . . Um. I could catch a fish and you could pull it off the hook or something."

"Uh-uh. No, siree. They're so wiggly and slimy."

They kept walking.

"Alright, I'll think about it. In the meantime, why don't you just focus on being brave today — getting donations and stuff. You ask, okay?"

"Um . . ."

Ugh. It sounded horrible, so Kate didn't actually agree outright. They rounded the corner and turned onto Broad Street, then crossed to the other side. Kate could just make out the florist at the end of the block. Her stomach clutched nervously in anticipation. It wouldn't be easy, even with Hillary there.

"Isn't there any other way to do it?" she asked, distracting herself from the upcoming donation scenario.

"No," said Hillary. "Let's just get it over with. You just walk in. . . ."

But Kate had stopped. Hanging from a second-story window above White's was a tiny sign she'd never noticed before. It was beautiful: hand-painted on wood, white with periwinkle blue lettering, and it said: PORTRAITS BY EDITH MUNSFIELD.

"Look!" said Kate, gesturing to the sign. "An artist!"

"Hey!" Hillary smiled winningly after reading the sign. "That would be cool! A painting!"

"Oh dear." *Why did I have to open my big mouth?* thought Kate. "I didn't mean it that way! I just meant, 'Look, isn't that cute?'" said Kate.

"Still," said Hillary.

They stood outside the building debating whether they should go in. Kate felt they shouldn't bother an artist who might be working, or in the middle of something important. Hillary saw it as an opportunity to raise more money for the clinic. Finally Hillary won when she played on Kate's heartstrings.

"What if she's just sitting up there, lonely, waiting for someone to call?"

"Oh, for heaven's sake! Fine!" Kate couldn't bear the thought. But as the name sunk in, it kind of rang a bell. *Edith Munsfield. Edith Munsfield,* she repeated to herself. Huh.

They climbed the steps to the porch and crossed over to the door in the corner that had her name above it. Then they opened the door to a steep wooden staircase that seemed to rise forever, and began the trek.

At the top of the stairs, Kate was winded, but Hillary was fine. There was a door with a glass panel to their right that said EDITH MUNSFIELD on it in gold lettering. But suddenly, Kate panicked.

"Wait. What are we going to say?" she whispered desperately.

Hillary shrugged. "I don't know. We'll just talk to her," she said in a normal voice.

"Shhh!" said Kate. "She'll hear you!"

"Hello?" called a voice from inside. "Is somebody there?"

It was too late. The door opened before they had a chance to reply, and before Kate even had a chance to compose herself, a woman stood before them, her hand on the knob.

Kate was taken aback. The woman was not what she had pictured. About eighty-something years old, with jet-back hair pulled into a bun at the back of her head, she was tall and strong-looking, with broad shoulders, a stout bosom like a pigeon, and a long floor-length black skirt. She wore a high-necked, long-sleeved pleated blouse, with a cameo at her throat, and a pair of tortoise-shell reading glasses low on her nose. She definitely did not look like an artist. She didn't even look like she belonged in this century!

"Yes?" said the woman.

Hillary found her voice first. "Hello. We're looking for Edith Munsfield."

"I am Miss Munsfield," said the woman without smiling.

Every image she'd ever seen of strict schoolmarms came flooding back into Kate's mind. For that was what Miss Munsfield looked like. And acted like. Kate was terrified.

"Um. We are here because we're collecting donations for the Sheehan Clinic Benefit . . . ," Hillary began.

Miss Munsfield began to close the door. "I do not give money to door-to-door solicitors. Send me a letter."

"Wait!" Hillary was undeterred. "We're not asking for money. It's for the auction and raffle. We're asking local businesses to donate things that could be sold or raffled off."

Miss Munsfield narrowed her eyes. But she reopened the door a bit. "How do I know you're legitimate?"

Kate's big blue eyes were round with fear. This was a disaster! But Hillary pressed on.

"You don't. But we are." She smiled. "I'm Hillary Callahan, and this is my cousin Kate. Our great-grandparents, the Sheehans, founded the clinic, and our grandmother Gee — I mean, Samantha Callahan — hosts the benefit at her house every year. This year they're behind on getting donations, so we're helping."

Kate looked from Hillary to Miss Munsfield. It was working. She could see Miss Munsfield softening a bit.

"I've heard of your grandmother, but I'm new to the island. I've never been to the clinic. Anyhow, I can't stand here all day. Why don't you come in?" She pulled the door open farther and stepped back to allow the girls in.

Wow! Kate was impressed. Hillary had saved the day! And all by being forthright and friendly, and just pressing on. The girls began to enter the studio, for that was what it was.

"Wait!" barked Miss Munsfield. "Your shoes!"

Mortified, Kate and Hillary stooped to remove their sneakers and leave them by the door.

"Now, do come in," said Miss Munsfield. "But don't touch anything!"

Kate was traumatized by Miss Munsfield's manner, but she followed her orders like a robot. There was no possibility of doing otherwise.

Inside, everything was so neat and bright that Kate winced. The floor was painted high-gloss bright white, and the walls and ceiling were white, too, with big skylights in the sloping roof. There was a stack of stretched canvases aligned in height order against the wall, like soldiers heading into battle. Against another wall was a glass-fronted steel medical cabinet full of perfectly neat jars and tubes of paint, and another clean glass jar full of immaculate paintbrushes. There wasn't a stray drop of paint anywhere to be seen. In fact, it looked more like a surgeon's office than an artist's studio.

But the walls were hung with the most precise, gorgeous paintings Kate had ever seen. In fact, she gasped aloud and rushed to the nearest wall to get a closer look.

Kate did a bit of painting on her own, but mostly in watercolors, which were loose and more tolerant of her beginner techniques. She couldn't imagine what a steady hand and sharp eye Edith Munsfield must have to be able to paint so perfectly. The portraits were of people and houses, stacked one above the other in pairs. The images were nearly photorealistic, but each had a beauty and an essence that kept them from being creepy or overly perfect, as most photorealistic painting was. Kate looked more closely. The brush strokes were invisible, but the detail was amazing! You could see a tear in that man's eye, so real you wanted to reach out and wipe it away! And the shingles on his house! Each one looked so perfect and individual!

Kate wheeled around, breathless with excitement. "How do you do it?" she cried, clapping her hands together. "It's like magic!"

Miss Munsfield pursed her lips to try to hide a pleased smile, but she failed. The smile lifted the corners of her mouth, and her eyes danced merrily despite herself. *She looks better when she smiles,* Kate realized. *Younger.*

"Thank you," said Miss Munsfield primly. "I do try."

Kate turned enthusiastically back to the paintings, all thoughts of donations far behind her.

Hillary, awkwardly out of her element, began to sit down on a small black couch in the corner. Miss Munsfield spied her out of the corner of her eye. "Wait!" she barked. Hillary froze, midway into her seat, as Miss Munsfield rushed over and laid a sheet of plastic for Hillary to sit on.

Hillary perched tentatively on the plastic-covered couch while Kate inspected the paintings further, one by one.

Miss Munsfield came to stand beside Kate, describing each one. Or rather each pair, because Miss Munsfield's current enthusiasm was painting portraits of houses and then their owners, and showing the two together. She relaxed as she described the works and their subjects, and Kate was absorbed in her descriptions, asking questions and pumping her for details on her technique and references.

Miss Munsfield was impressed by Kate's knowledge, as Kate pulled out art terminology that she hadn't even remembered learning, like *vanishing point* and *contraposto*. She'd had an art history course in school that year, with piles of slides of old masters and other famous works of art, and, of course, she'd always been artistic, immersing herself in books on painting technique and asking in-depth questions in her art classes at school. Her paintings always hung prominently in the student art show at the end of each school year, but she considered herself a dabbler, since art came third on her list of passions, after baking and home-making crafts like needlework and decorating; she'd never think to call herself an artist. But Kate was energized by their discussion, and the time flew by as they walked around the studio. From time to time she'd glance at Hillary, trying to figure out if Hillary minded her wasting their time like this, and hoping that she didn't; but Hillary's slack-jawed expression was one of rapt surprise — she was taking in every word.

Finally, things were wrapping up. Miss Munsfield folded her hands together and wrung them in total joy. "This has been the most wonderful afternoon since my arrival on Gull. Truly exceptional! I simply cannot believe that I have finally met someone on Gull who has the same interests and pastimes as I do."

Kate beamed and glanced at Hillary, who was staring at her in wonder.

"Now, about the auction," continued Miss Munsfield. She looked at Hillary, but Hillary looked at Kate, so Miss Munsfield turned back to Kate. "What shall I donate?"

"Oh!" Kate was caught off-guard. "Um . . . well, you don't really need to . . ."

"Nonsense!" said Miss Munsfield, back to her stern self. "After the time I've spent with you I'm prepared to be very generous. In addition, you've seen that flight of stairs I have to climb each day. If I were to take a tumble, I'd certainly want the people at the clinic to know that I am a supporter of theirs." She crossed the room briskly to an old-fashioned rolltop desk, and furled the cover with a clackety clatter. Inside, the desk was arranged as neatly as the rest of the studio: pens aligned in rows, stamps neatly curled in a bowl, and note cards and envelopes slotted tidily into the pigeonholes. She withdrew a card, an envelope, and a beautiful fountain pen; Kate spied a monogram at the top of the periwinkle-blue-bordered card: *E.T.M.* Then Miss Munsfield sat down on the caned swivel chair with a sweep of her skirt and began to make out the card.

When she'd finished, she fanned it in the air so that the ink would dry (Kate was half-expecting her to use a blotter and some sealing wax with a stamp to seal the envelope). Then she slid the card into the envelope and handed it to Kate brusquely.

"Here. I hope someone bids on it," she said modestly.

"Oh, Miss Munsfield, I'm sure they will," said Kate enthusiastically, not knowing what it could be. Paints? A sketch of your house, done from a photograph? Suddenly, something in Miss Munsfield's profile looked familiar to Kate, and the familiarity of her name and the image of her at her desk came rushing together into a memory. Kate gasped.

"You're E. Tillinghast Munsfield!" she cried, her hand pressed to her chest in shock.

Miss Munsfield turned to her and smiled. "Yes."

E. Tillinghast Munsfield was one of the greatest painters of a group that had included many of the top names of the mid-twentieth century. Unable to make a go of a career in art as a woman in the early days, Munsfield had exhibited under her middle and last name, so that people would assume she was a man. Once her reputation was secured — for she was a brilliant and ultimately well-known artist — she came out of hiding and revealed herself to be a woman. Kate had studied her in school, she now realized, and she and her mother had seen her work hanging in the Metropolitan Museum in New York City! Kate couldn't believe it! She was thrilled, and mortified!

"I had no idea! I mean, I didn't put two and two together! I am *so* sorry to have bothered you!" Kate started backing out of the room.

Miss Munsfield smiled again, kindly, and waved her back. "There's no need to apologize, dear girl. I have spent more than enough time in my life with people who *do* know who I am, and I can tell you that there is nothing more boring than being revered and respected — people whispering in my presence and acting like I am some kind of goddess. I am just a painter — someone who can use oil and pigment to put together a representation of real-life objects on canvas, albeit in a somewhat unique way. I just happen to have figured out my interests at a very young age, and thus gave myself quite a head start in my apprenticeships and the practicing of my skills. And, of course, in the publicizing of my name and my work." She held her hands out in a kind of an apologetic shrug. "I've been doing this since I was a child myself. It's really just child's play, all grown up," she added with a wink. "Some of us are fortunate enough to know what we love and who we are from quite a young age."

Kate nodded, embarrassed. "Well, we won't keep you any longer, Miss Munsfield. Thank you so much for your time." Kate's face was scarlet with excitement and embarrassment, and she waved for Hillary to come along. She was bursting and she couldn't wait to get outside so she could talk with Hillary in private. Plus she couldn't fathom taking up any more of Miss Munsfield's time. The girls jammed their sneakers back onto their feet.

"It was a most refreshing visit, girls, and I thank you," said Miss Munsfield.

The two thanked Miss Munsfield again profusely, and among her earnest entreaties for them to return, they backed out the door issuing assurances and gratitude, and tromped back down the stairs. Neither exchanged a word until they were well down the block. Then they collapsed onto a weather-smoothed wooden bench by mutual unspoken agreement. A bird chirped in the tree above them, *wheep, wheep, wheep!*

"Wow," said Hillary, shaking her head.

"I know," said Kate, staring blindly down at the grass grow-ing through the cracks in the sidewalk, her eyes wide. "I can't believe that was her. I wonder why she's living here?"

"No, you, I mean!" protested Hillary. "Wow to you!"

"Thanks. I wonder what she gave us," said Kate, scrubbing the grass with the toe of her sneaker. She was still in shock. It hadn't even sunk in that she'd just secured another donation. It had been too easy. And fun, once it got going. Plus, she was with Hillary, and Hillary was the one who had started it off. It wasn't like Kate had done it all alone — not nearly as scary. Anyway, they'd met a major celebrity, and that was what had colored the whole experience for Kate.

"I'm not talking about the donation, you dope!" said Hillary, punching Kate playfully in the arm.

"Ow!" protested Kate, rubbing her arm and snapping out of her trance.

"I didn't hit you that hard. Don't be a baby. Anyway, I'm talking about you, and art, and the things you know, and all that. It was amazing! I had no idea you knew so much!" Hillary's eyes were wide again with amazement — she had the same look on her face that Kate had noticed when they were still in the studio.

Kate waved her compliment away. "Oh, that's nothing. I've just . . . I'm interested in art, is all. My mom takes me to museums in the city and stuff. You know." Kate shrugged. Trips to the city to see art were fairly common in her family, even though she had slightly exaggerated their frequency to Sloan on the beach that day. She hadn't admitted that that was why they went, since it sounded so dorky, but it was true. Her mom loved art, and sometimes her dad would sneak away from work for a bit to come meet them for a quick tour and some lunch.

"Well, you really know how to talk the talk," said Hillary. "I couldn't believe you in there. It was like you were someone I didn't even know!"

"Thanks," said Kate. And then in a whisper she said, "Hey, do you think we could look at what she donated?" She hefted the thick white envelope in her hand and tried to peer down the side. Miss Munsfield hadn't sealed it.

Hillary shrugged. "Sure."

Kate slid the card out. It read: "One portrait, in oil." And it was signed, *Edith T. Munsfield.*

"Wow," breathed Kate. "That is serious! *Seriously* serious! I mean, even having her signature on this *card* is serious!"

"And all because of you!" said Hillary.

"No," protested Kate.

"Yes," said Hillary firmly. And then, "She was a little strange, wasn't she? And that all-white place of hers?"

"Uh-huh," agreed Kate with a giggle. "You know, she's famous for her clean studio. It's like, her trademark. People used to not believe she painted her paintings herself, because her studio was so clean, but she did. Then, a lot of feminists in the sixties got all mad because they said for a famous female painter, she shouldn't spend so much time on her housekeeping." Kate giggled again. "But it turns out that she thinks through the whole painting while she cleans, before she even starts to paint. And also, if there's even one thing astray in her studio, she gets so distracted she can't even work. So that's why her studio looked like that."

"Weird," said Hillary, looking off down the street. A puffy white cloud floated by, washing the two in shadow and then passing to let the sun beam back down again. Hillary was already itching to move on — the encounter hadn't meant that much to her since she had no idea who E. Tillinghast Munsfield was — but Kate was still basking in the experience.

"Yeah," sighed Kate contentedly. Maybe she would go back and visit again. It had been so interesting. And she wanted to hear more about how Miss Munsfield had realized she was an artist from a very young age. That would be good to know. *Maybe I'll be an artist when I grow up*, thought Kate, conveniently shelving her plans to be a chef or a cookbook mogul. *That would be cool.*

Kate heaved herself to her feet and stowed the envelope in the file she was now keeping in her tote bag to hold her scant donations (Old Mill, Summer Reading, Gullboutique, now this). She groaned as she hoisted the heavy bag onto her shoulder and set out for their next stop, the florist, finally.

"You know, you should give that *bag* a makeover," said Hillary with a sly grin.

"What do you mean?" Kate liked her bag. Anyway, it was the same as the other girls'.

"Ditch, like, ninety percent of the stuff in there, for starters," said Hillary. "It can't be good for your back or your posture to carry that stuff around all the time."

"But I need this stuff!" Kate grimaced as the straps cut into her shoulder. It did weigh a ton, she had to admit.

Hillary shrugged. "Maybe you just think you do."

"You need it, too, you know!" snapped Kate. "It's got the sunscreen, and the Band-Aids, and snacks, and . . . everything."

Hillary looked at her, dead-on. "You don't have to take care of everyone all the time, you know."

Kate was taken aback. "I . . . Yes, I do!"

They'd arrived outside the Enchanted Forest, the town's only flower shop (save for the hand-picked bouquets of brightly colored zinnias and other hardy flowers that the farm stands all sold), and were facing each other.

Hillary softened. "I'm not trying to be mean. I just feel bad for you, all weighted down and stuff. I could help you sift through it later, if you like," she offered kindly.

"Thanks," said Kate. But she knew she wouldn't take Hillary up on her offer. She liked having her stuff with her. It made her feel safe.

They climbed the two stone steps to the florist's door and went inside.

CHAPTER FIFTEEN

Floral Designer

$\mathscr{T}$he door closed behind them with a hush and a squeaky sealing sound. The air was thick with the smell of hothouse flowers, and nearly freezing cold — Kate could see her breath. Tinkly New Age music was piping in from somewhere, and a little fountain in the corner babbled soothingly. Kate inhaled deeply and smiled. This was her kind of place. All around her were the most fantastic creations of floral and greenery: a little log cabin of sticks sat on a garden of moss, with flowers acting as tiny shrubs and trees around it — a miniature home fit for a fairy, the whole thing not more than one square foot in total; nearby was a large high heel created out of bright red roses stuffed into chicken wire; a gorgeous silver urn spilled forth grapes, roses, vines, and persimmons in a still life worthy of one of Miss Munsfield's paintings. Kate couldn't believe her eyes. This wasn't just a florist — it was another artist's studio.

"Hello!" called Hillary, snapping Kate out of her reverie.

"Hel-lo! Be-right-there!" trilled a high male voice from the back of the store, his words quick and light and all in a rush.

The cousins looked at each other, and then the elf came bounding out. Or at least, that was what Kate thought at first. He was about forty years old and tiny — smaller than she; petite, like a jockey. He had bright red hair, truly green eyes, and milky-white skin, as if he never went outside except during a full moon. But his smile was as wide as his face, from ear to ear, and his elastic lips and big white teeth (*fake?* wondered Kate distractedly) were charming and inviting in their smile, and Kate and Hillary smiled back, nearly giggling at his contagious energy.

He stopped abruptly right in front of them and put his hands on his hips. He seemed to vibrate, even at a standstill, as if he had a million projects to do and couldn't possibly stand in one place for even a moment. In fact, a millisecond after he stopped moving he began again, fussily rearranging the fairy's house, then neatening up the high heel, picking off dead rose petals that were visible only to his eyes. But he kept smiling at them engagingly. "What can I do for you?" he asked. He spoke so quickly that it took a second for Kate to register what he'd even said. Hillary was still staring blankly at him, so Kate spoke up, embarrassed for their staring.

She cleared her throat. "We're here about the benefit for the clinic . . ."

"Oh, right, right, uh-huh, yup. All righty. I know all about it. I'm all ready. Signed up. *Signed, sealed, delivered, I'm yours,*" he sang in a high falsetto. Kate laughed in spite of herself.

"You mean you gave at the office?" she prodded, in a way that was most unlike her. Something about this tiny man made her feel gregarious and confident, and she wanted to joke around with him.

"You could say that, Mac." He danced a little shuffle. "*Everything's coming up roses,*" he sang loudly, and he scattered the rose petals in the air, where they floated gently to the polished stone floor. Then he bent down on one knee and flung his arms open wide. "I'm in a show tune mood today. What do you want to hear?"

Kate and Hillary looked at each other, laughing. Was this guy for real?

"Uh, 'Chitty Chitty Bang Bang'?" suggested Kate.

"*That's Right, Chitty Chitty Bang Bang, Chitty Chitty Bang Bang we love you!*" sang the man in a gorgeous voice. Then, "Too easy," he said. "Give me something harder."

"*Phantom of the Opera,*" said Kate. She'd loved that one. She'd seen it on Broadway with her parents and her siblings, and she'd seen the movie, too. The man began singing "All I Ask of You," and before Kate knew what had happened, he was gesturing for her to take the female lead, and the two of them were singing at the top of their lungs in a perfect duet. They carried it through to the end (Kate knew all the words by heart from the CD in her dad's car, because she often sang it with him on the way to school in the mornings if he dropped her off), and wound up with her on his knee, cheeks pressed together, and Hillary clapping and crying with laughter, across the store.

Breathless, they stood. He bowed and held her hand, gesturing for her to curtsy.

"So. Nate Spangleman. Pleased to meet you, little lady. You've got some set of pipes there. Whew!" He yanked a paper towel off the roll on the counter and mopped his sweating face, then he offered the damp paper to Kate. "For your scrapbook?" he said.

She looked at it, grossed out for a split second, and he laughed, pulling it away. "*Kid*-ding!" he said. "Here," and he handed her a fresh one. She was surprised to see that she, too, was sweating.

Hillary had caught her breath. "That was so good, you guys! I swear! Like, professional!"

Nate grimaced at Kate. "Fans. So annoying, really. Waiting outside the stage door, following you to dinner after the show. Ah, comes with the territory, I guess. Gee, you really can sing, kiddo!"

Kate laughed again. "Thanks."

"She can, can't she!" Hillary beamed with pride. "We keep telling her that."

"Who's we? Are there a whole bunch more of you outside in the family bus or something?"

"Nah, just two more . . . at large. Wandering the island," said Hillary. "How did you know we were related?"

"The eyes. Mrs. Callahan's eyes. I'd know 'em a mile away. Penetrating. Gorgeous. Refreshing. Like a cold pool on a hot summer's day."

Kate and Hillary smiled at each other in surprise. "How do you know our grandmother?" asked Kate.

"She's one of my best customers. Or, recipients, I should say. She probably gets sent more flowers than anyone else on the island. It's coals to Newcastle, I always say, since she'd got that gorgeous cutting garden out there. But people are always wanting to send her something to thank her. It challenges me. I'm running out of ideas for her. I can't bring the same thing each time, you know." He leaned in and looked at them mock-seriously. "She'd kill me and eat me for dinner."

Kate nodded solemnly. "That's what happened to the last florist." Hillary looked at Kate in surprise at her humor and laughed.

"Florist! Florist! I'm not a florist! I'm a designer, who happens to use God's living bounty as his medium! Florist! Yuck!" Nate pretended to spit on the floor. Kate would've been embarrassed, but she could tell he was joking.

Nate leaned in close. "It's so much more than flowers, baby."

"I see," said Kate.

Nate crossed his arms. "When I was a kid, yes. 'Florist' would've sufficed. I was in Natick, Mass., doing real FTD kind of work. Bouquets in bowls with tacky baby's breath, and little plastic signs popping out that said, 'Baby Boy!' and 'Mazel Tov!' But once I got a taste of Newbury Street, it was goodbye, Charlie. I became a floral designer. An *artiste!*" He kissed his fingers and flung them into the air.

"So you've been a, uh, floral designer for how long?" asked Kate.

Nate counted on his fingers, rapidly ticking off the years. "Four hundred and twenty-two years, if you count leap years."

"Oh," Kate smiled.

"So what can I do for you little Callahans today?" asked Nate.

"Well . . ." Kate glanced at Hillary, and Hillary nodded, gesturing for Kate to ask. *What the heck?* thought Kate. *It's been a great afternoon. What do I have to lose?* So she spoke quickly, just like Nate. "We're collecting donations for the clinic benefit auction and raffle. And we were wondering . . . if, maybe . . ."

"Sure. You betcha. Love to, kid. Love giving away free stuff. Good for the heart. What did you have in mind?" Nate went to stand by the tall floral-arranging counter, and propped his elbow on its surface and rested his chin in his hand. His other hand drummed out a rhythm on the counter. He started to hum. All of this in one second flat.

"Um." Kate spun in a slow circle, looking around the store. "Do you sell nursery stock, too?"

Nate nodded and jammed his thumb toward the rear of the store. "Out back."

"Then, some roses? Pink? Like, maybe Old Blush? Or a hydrangea bush? Heliotrope?"

Hillary glanced at her like she was speaking a foreign language.

"Could do that. Could offer a garden makeover."

"Complete with fertilizer?" prodded Kate. Hillary was now staring at her.

"With a side order of aphid killer?"

"Only if it's organic," countered Kate with a grin.

"Annuals or perennials?"

"Come on! Don't be a cheapskate!" Kate shook her finger at him.

"How about some root conditioner?"

"Only lime for hydrangeas."

"Ha! Nearly gotcha on that one!" Nate and Kate laughed companionably.

Finally Hillary interrupted. "What are you two *talking* about?"

Kate turned to her and smiled. "Gardening."

Hillary shook her head. "It sounded like Greek to me."

"Lovely gardens in Greece this time of year," said Nate with a fake fancy accent.

Kate turned back to Nate. "Maybe you should just donate, like, a floral fantasy, delivered to your home . . . once a week! For the whole summer!"

"Girlfriend, you're trying to run me out of business!"

"Come on! It could be great!" Kate couldn't believe she was pressing this man or elf or whatever he was. It was so unlike her. She felt like she was floating above herself, watching someone else take over her body and speak, using her voice.

Nate stared out the store window for a minute. "Ah, fine! You got me. I'll do it." Then he shook his finger at Kate. "But you're coming to bail me out if I go bankrupt on this one. Get it?"

"Well, just use a lot of fruit. It's cheaper than flowers."

"Ho-ho! Listen to the child prodigy!" Nate gestured at Kate and wiggled his eyebrows at Hillary. "Don't bring her next time," he stage-whispered to Hillary. "She's got it in for me. Wants to see me suffer."

"Deal," Hillary whispered back.

The girls then watched as Nate rummaged in his desk for a gift certificate to fill out. He hummed to himself, and Kate picked up the tune — another Broadway song — and began humming in harmony along with him. Meanwhile, he filled out the pink card and handed it over with a flourish.

"Don't say I never gave you anything," he cautioned jokingly.

"I'd never," said Kate, eyes opened wide in innocence.

"Thank you, Mr. Spangleman," said Hillary.

"Call me Nate, kid. Nate the Great." He ruffled Hillary's hair, having to reach up to do it.

"Thanks," said Kate warmly. "That was really generous of you."

"Yes, well, when I'm in the poorhouse, come and visit me." He followed the girls to the door. "And bring me treats. *Good* ones. Like *Hello!* Magazine and Lilac Chocolates. The other inmates will be so impressed!"

The girls left the store laughing, and he stood at the door waving for a moment as they walked away up the block.

"Katie, you are too much!" said Hillary admiringly.

Kate was dying of thirst after all that singing. "Why?" She smiled, knowing why. She'd had fun, and she couldn't believe it. It made her want to keep going, keep asking for more donations.

"The singing, and the flower talk, and forcing him to give such a generous donation! Is it really you in there?" Hillary stopped to stare intently into Kate's eyes, and Kate waved her away, laughing.

"I need to get a Coke before we keep going," she said.

"Keep going?" Hillary looked around incredulously. "Where else is there to go? And anyway, a Coke?"

"Oh. Yeah." Kate paused. "What should I drink?" she asked sadly. All of her little treats were being taken away from her, and she felt sad.

"How about water?" suggested Hillary.

"Oh yeah. *Water!*" said Kate, like she'd never had it before. "Do you think they sell water at the Fudge Co.?"

They crossed Broad Street, went into the store, and Hillary stood aside while Kate selected a bottle of water from the fridge. Kate was still feeling bold after their encounter with Nate, so before she could help herself, she asked, "Hi. Have you already made a donation to the Health Clinic benefit?"

The girl paused and said, "Yes. Yup, we have. A girl with long blond hair came in and got something from the owner yesterday."

Kate and Hillary smiled at each other. "Phoebe," said Hillary.

"Alright, then. Thank you."

"Anything else I can help you with?" the girl asked pleasantly.

Kate stared longingly at the case of fudge. Finally she tore her eyes away. "Nope. Just this." She plunked the water on the counter and paid.

Outside, they paused for Kate to have a long sip of her water.

"Listen," Hillary began. "Aside from your terrible eating habits, I don't think there's a lot you need to do in the make-over department anymore."

Kate was surprised. "But I'm still a chicken, and an old lady and stuff."

"Not so much," said Hillary. "Not today, anyway. Look at you asking for a fudge donation all on your own!" They reached their bikes and began stashing their bags in the baskets for the ride home.

"Well, today was different. I got mad at Gullboutique, and that made me be brave about Sloan and letting her pierce my ear. Then the ear piercing made me braver about getting donations or something. I don't know. But I think . . . it's like . . . one brave thing leads to another, or something, you know?"

"Yeah." Hillary climbed onto her bike, and Kate did the same. "Yeah, like you get more confident, so you do new stuff, and that makes you more confident, and it just keeps building. It's like that in skiing."

Kate shrugged. "I guess. I'm a terrible skier. I'd rather stay in the lodge and drink cocoa. But I know what you mean."

They were silent for a minute, and then Kate added, "You know, maybe because Miss Munsfield and Nate both do things that I love — art and flowers — which are still old-ladyish, but maybe because I could speak their language, I felt kind of safe with them. Like . . ." — she searched for the word and was surprised as it rolled off her tongue — ". . . secure."

Hillary nodded. "I know what you mean. Like when I talk sports with people, I'm in my element. I don't ever feel shy or insecure."

"Yeah, I was in my element! That's what it was."

They smiled at each other, pleased that they'd figured it out. And then they rode home, eager to see the others, and Gee, and tell them about the experiences they'd had that afternoon.

CHAPTER SIXTEEN

The Salon, Again

"Okay," said Kate, wincing. She took a deep breath. "Okay. I'm ready. I think." Then she closed her eyes.

Neeve held the pencil in her hand and angled it up Kate's face, from the corner of her nose to the middle of her eyebrow. Neeve's own eyebrows were furrowed in concentration. "It's just . . ." She glanced at the open fashion magazine on her bed. "The arch is supposed to line up like this . . . and the end is supposed to be here . . . okay. I think I've got it." She dropped the pencil on the bed and picked up the tweezers.

"Ready?"

"Ready."

And Neeve touched one hair, and Kate's eyes flew open. "OW!" she screamed, clasping her hand to her eyebrow. "That really hurt!"

"You have to get used to it," said Neeve calmly. "Beauty hurts."

Phoebe glanced up from her bed, where she was reading *Anna Karenina*. Kate couldn't imagine why someone would read that book in their own free time. "Daphne always ices her eyebrow first." Daphne was Phoebe's older sister, and as fashionable as Phoebe wasn't.

"Hills, ice me, baby," said Neeve.

"All the way up there?" Hillary was doing her stretches and was clearly not psyched to run up to the kitchen in the main house for ice.

"It's for a good cause," said Kate, whimpering.

"I'll go," offered Lark, who was sleeping over. Neeve and Phoebe had run into her in town, and invited her over for dinner and a sleepover. Kate was put out when she arrived home — she'd been looking forward to telling the others about the time she and Hillary had had, but Lark's presence made her feel self-conscious, like she couldn't brag or ham it up. So the story got told by Hillary, who kept forgetting important parts. Then Lark had monopolized Gee's attention at the dinner table, as Gee asked her all sorts of questions about her early childhood in Japan, and her parents' work as marine biology researchers at Harvard (they were on a research sabbatical, living on Gull for two years to track something about seaweed that Kate found gross and boring). Kate was frustrated. And now Lark was sleeping over, and Kate was embarrassed that Lark was witnessing stage two of her makeover. She'd tried to postpone it, but Hillary had gotten the others — especially Neeve — geared up for it, and they wouldn't let her back down. After all, they didn't have any other plans for the evening.

Kate sighed in irritation as Lark went bounding out of the Dorm.

"What's the matter?" asked Neeve.

"Nothing," said Kate. "Just that I wasn't planning on having strangers in the audience."

"Lark's not a stranger!" said Neeve in surprise.

"More or less," muttered Kate. She lifted her index finger and smoothed her thick eyebrows. She hoped Neeve knew what she was doing, but she was willing to go along with it because she felt like the new haircut had helped her out so much — made her braver, even if it got her into a little trouble. Maybe new eyebrows would help her be even braver. Plus, it was fun to have Neeve's attention focused on her.

Lark returned and, moments later, the ice was melting uncomfortably on Kate's brow, and Neeve was flipping through the magazine for "eyebrow ideas."

"Hey, should we do color tonight while we're at it?" suggested Neeve brightly. Kate considered this for a moment and then shrugged. Why not? Her earlobe smarted, and felt hot to the touch now, but it wasn't too bad. Just enough pain to remind her she'd been brave enough to try the piercing in the first place.

"Okay, I guess."

And then, with Kate's agreement still hanging in the air, Neeve was all business, locating the hair color ("Good. Semi-permanent!" she said, reading the box), setting up a chair, grabbing her comb, and bustling around. She'd do the color first and then pluck Kate's eyebrows while the color set.

Lark watched the process closely, eyes wide with wonder. Every once in a while she'd say something like, "Wow, Neeve. You're really good at this. How did you learn so much about hair?" and Kate would roll her eyes while Neeve ate it up. Lark was such a brown-noser. It was annoying and pathetic the way she just worshipped Neeve and even the others to a lesser extent. Kate sat in her chair, her hair in Neeve's hands and the tangy smell of hair dye hanging in the air, and thought uncharitable thoughts. Like that Lark should get a life.

"Hey, Neeve?" asked Lark finally.

"Mm-hmm?"

"Would you, um, is there any possible way that maybe, if it's not too much trouble, you'd, like, do my hair one time if I got some dye?"

Kate rolled her eyes for the tenth time.

Neeve was thrilled. "Totally!" She dropped her hands from Kate's head and wiped the dye solution on an old towel. Then she leaned over and fluffed Lark's hair around in an annoyingly (to Kate) professional manner. She lifted it and let it drop a few times, then mussed it around, turning Lark's head this way and that, chattering about cut and color.

"Uh, hello? I've got dye on my hair over here? Let's not forget what we're doing!" Kate fumed.

Neeve glanced at her, distracted by Lark's head of long black hair — a blank canvas for Neeve's sudden hairdressing skills. "What?"

"Remember me? My hair's going to fall out if you leave this stuff on too long. Plus, you still need to do my eyebrows, and the ice is nearly all melted."

"Oh. Right." Neeve returned to Kate and looked at her watch. "Ten more minutes. Why don't you ice up those brows and I'll do a bit now."

Kate shifted in her seat, irritated but pleased that Neeve's attention had returned to its proper place. She iced her eyebrow for a minute, then blotted it dry and looked up at Neeve. Neeve had the tweezers in her hand, and she leaned in close to begin the plucking. Kate steeled herself against the pain, but the first one hurt so much she gasped. She slid her eyes over to Lark, and saw Lark's expression of sympathy.

"Wow, Kate! You are so brave! I could never stand the pain!" said Lark.

Kate gritted her teeth as Neeve continued. No way was she going to let Lark see how much it hurt. No way. Lark watched them, a look of absorption on her face, and tears began to form in Kate's eyes — just from the pain, not because she was crying, thank you very much.

Finally, Kate couldn't stand being stared at anymore. "Lark, isn't there something else you could do besides watch me?" she said, not in the nicest way.

Lark was mortified. "Oh. Sorry. Right." She looked around the room for something to do.

Neeve had watched the exchange silently, and now she gave Kate a dirty look. "Lark-o, you can go ahead and try on those things of mine we were talking about. It's all in the bottom drawer right there."

Lark-o? thought Kate. *That's a new one.*

"Thanks!" said Lark happily. She slid off the bed and went to Neeve's dresser to rummage. Meanwhile, the plucking continued, and now Kate's eyebrow was stinging, on its way to throbbing. She watched Lark out of her good eye, keeping the other one closed under Neeve's hand.

Lark took a handful of things into the bathroom, closed the door to change, and emerged a moment later in one of Neeve's outrageous get-ups: zebra-striped leggings, a green tulle mini-skirt, a shredded tank top, and a blackwatch plaid vest over it all. She stood in the doorway and said shyly, "What do you think?"

Neeve dropped her hands from Kate's face and raced across the room to examine Lark. "Oh. My. God. You look amazing! Here, spin around."

Kate watched in mounting anger as Phoebe and Hillary

looked up and smiled. Lark did look amazing. It was true. Everyone began fawning over her, and she blushed furiously from the attention, but, Kate noticed, she loved it.

Kate stood up from her seat and brushed past the group now huddled just in front of the bathroom doorway. "I've had enough of this hair dye thing," she said to no one. She went into the bathroom and looked in the mirror. She looked like a total weirdo: shower cap on her head; deep red dye along her hairline, and one half-plucked eyebrow that actually looked sort of alarming — the skin fiery red and inflamed and, where it was plucked, sort of naked. She slammed the door to the bathroom, not caring what the others thought; hoping, in fact, that they'd know she was mad. She pulled off the shower cap and took off her clothes, starting the shower in the meantime. Then she got in and washed her hair, watching the red dye swirl down the drain. It probably wouldn't take now — there was some sort of procedure she was supposed to follow to make sure it stayed in her hair, but she didn't care. Neeve had a new guinea pig in Lark, and she could do whatever she wanted to her, thought Kate, conveniently forgetting that she'd been the one who'd originally asked for a makeover, not the other way around.

She emerged, dripping and toweled off, checking to make sure that the dye didn't come off on one of the towels. Then she looked at herself closely in the mirror. With her hair wet, it was hard to tell if the color had worked, but she could detect a definite redness around the edges. Her eyebrow was a problem, though. Neeve would have to finish it and do the other one to match; there was no way to stop once she'd started, or she'd look lopsided and freaky. Kate sighed. She wasn't as mad now as she'd been when she'd gotten into the shower. Just annoyed. She opened the door to the bathroom and was ready to announce her new hair color to the others, but instead she simply stood there, aghast, her hand on the door handle.

Lark was in her seat, dressed in Neeve's clothes, her head tipped back while Neeve brandished the tweezers above Lark's eyebrows.

"What are you doing?!" cried Kate.

Everyone looked at her. "Lark's eyebrows," said Neeve, stating the obvious.

"But you're supposed to be doing *mine!*" whined Kate, embarrassed by her tone but too mad to care.

"Sorry!" said Lark, jumping up. "Sorry! Here you go!" She waved Kate over to the chair.

Kate was mad. She hated the way Lark always acted so nice and sympathetic, and made her seem like she was some witch. *She* was supposed to be the nice one!

"Oh, what*ever!*" spat Kate, in a most un-nice way.

"Kate!" said Hillary, shocked. "What's the deal?"

"The deal is that Lark is trying to, like, take over. And it's rude. And annoying!" Kate stormed across the room to her dresser and pulled a nightgown and underwear out, willy-nilly. Other stuff spilled out of the drawer onto the floor but she didn't stop to pick it up, the way she normally would've.

"Kate, you're the one who's being rude. And to our guest," said Phoebe. Lark was kind of cowering, looking like she wasn't sure where to go or what to do. Kate couldn't stand the sight of her anymore.

"She's not *my* guest. I didn't invite her!" Kate shot back.

"I think I should go," said Lark quietly.

"No!" said Neeve. She turned to Kate. "Kate, stop being so . . . aggressive."

"Aggressive? Aggressive?!" Kate was incredulous. "What are you talking about?" No one had ever, ever in her life called her aggressive.

Neeve shrugged. "I don't know. You're just not your usual self. You're all bossy and irritable, and you want to be the center of attention. It's just not like you." She wasn't mad-sounding, just matter-of-fact.

Everyone was watching them in silence. Kate didn't know what to say.

"Well . . ." Tears threatened, but she would not cry in front of Lark. She took a deep breath. "It's just, I feel like Lark's taking my place or something." And then the tears began to fall. She couldn't help it. It had been such a long day, and she'd pushed herself too hard. The ear piercing. The donations. And now another makeover. She was exhausted. It was really hard work trying to change.

She sat on her bed, still in her towel, and cried. Finally, Lark, of all of them, came and sat next to her. She put her hand on Kate's shoulder. "I'm sorry," she said quietly. "I know I've been forcing myself on you guys. And you've been so nice to me; especially you, Kate. . . ."

Kate winced. She didn't feel like she'd been especially nice to Lark. Not more than the others had. And she felt guilty now that Lark thought that her little crumbs of attention were the best she had to offer.

Lark continued. "It's just . . . I don't have any brothers or sisters. And I don't have any cousins here in the U.S. And I'm only living here for two years; my real friends are back in Cambridge, and I'm kind of stuck here. With Sloan. . . ." She drawled Sloan's name in a dead-on imitation of the way Sloan talked, and everyone laughed. Even Kate.

Lark smiled. "You guys are just so fun, and so cool. And there's always something going on here, because you're all together. It's like a permanent sleepover party. And you're always, like, baking something delicious — like those snacks you bring to clinic for everyone — or decorating, or doing some craft. And you're so good at all that stuff. And Neeve's so good at fashion stuff, and Phoebe's so smart — smarter than a lot of my really smart friends back home. And Hillary's so adventurous. And I'm . . . I just feel like a loser on Gull. Left out, and sort of out of my element. So it's really fun for me when you guys invite me to do stuff. And I know I seem desperate. But it's because I am. You're the only normal people I've hung out with since I got here."

Now Kate felt terrible. She wanted to hug Lark, but she felt weird since she was still in her towel. She looked around at the others, and they all had sympathetic looks on their faces. "I had no idea," she said to Lark helplessly.

Lark shrugged. "It's okay. I mean, it's not like I go around advertising that I feel like a loser. I just figured you, of all people, could tell."

Kate's temper flared again. "*I* could tell? Why? Because it takes one to know one? Is that it?"

Lark looked surprised. "No. Because you're so nice and kind to everyone. You're such a people person, and so secure. I just figured you were used to people looking up to you."

Lark's words were like a bucket of water, dousing Kate's anger. "I'm not secure! And *no one* looks up to me," she said, laughing dryly.

"I do," said Lark.

"Me too," added Hillary from across the room.

Kate scoffed. "Yeah. I'm sure."

"Come on, Kate! We all do," said Neeve. "You're so talented at so many things. Even adult things, like cooking and knitting . . ."

"And art and flowers . . ." added Hillary.

"And decorating!" added Neeve. Kate smiled; she and Neeve had really battled it out on the decorating front when they'd redone the Dorm.

"And taking care of people . . ." Hillary was still going.

"Okay, stop! Stop!" Kate was embarrassed. She looked at Lark. "I'm sorry I've been so mean."

"It was only tonight," said Lark. "And it's okay. You *didn't* invite me over."

"Still," said Kate. Embarrassment was creeping in. She shouldn't have been so rude to Lark. She looked down at her towel. "Let me go change," she said.

"I think you already have," said Hillary quietly.

"Yes," agreed Neeve. She nodded at Hillary.

"Really?" asked Kate, standing now.

"Uh-huh." Hillary was serious.

"Especially around the eyebrows!" cried Neeve. Everyone laughed.

"Yeah. You need to finish these up — even them out. Please. After you're done with Lark."

"No. You go first," said Lark. "Really. You started first."

"Okay. Thanks." Kate smiled.

"No, thank you," said Lark.

"You're welcome," said Kate, rising to go put on her clothes in the bathroom.

Lark's words had surprised Kate. She couldn't believe Lark thought she was cool, or secure! Especially since all the stuff she'd ever been secure about back home had been totally thrown into flux during her stay on Gull. She'd felt nothing but *insecure* and uncool these past few weeks. *But,* she rationalized, *Lark isn't exactly cool herself. Maybe she's just more of a loser than I am, so she thinks I'm cool or something.* Then she stopped herself. *Yet Sloan seems to think Lark is cool — or cool enough to hang out with, anyway. What does that mean?*

It was only later that Kate realized Phoebe hadn't said anything. Hadn't added to the list of nice things that everyone had said about Kate. Huh, thought Kate. Maybe she was just . . . but what? What was she just? Kate couldn't figure it out.

CHAPTER SEVENTEEN

Knitting Is Cool

The next day was unseasonably cool and breezy, but warm in the sun. Kate pulled her pink sweater around her shoulders more snugly and looked down at her notebook again. The others had ridden their bikes over to Lark's for a while. She had a new desk in her room and she needed help moving it and reimagining the layout of the room. Kate knew Lark had wanted her to come, but she'd felt a pleasant, if unfamiliar, surge of power in turning Lark down. She didn't do it to be mean; she'd just set her heart on getting organized this afternoon, and she really wanted some time to herself in which to do it.

She picked a bite of zucchini bread off the slice sitting beside her on a napkin. Yum. It was delicious. After what Lark had said about Kate bringing snacks to clinic, Kate had reassessed her strike. Her baking always brought joy to people — including herself. So why not keep on with it? She didn't have to make fattening or unhealthy things, either! So she'd baked up a batch of zucchini bread using an old recipe of Sheila's, and boxed up the slices to take to clinic the next day. Besides being delicious (almost as good as the farmer's wife's), it had been fun doing it; it felt great to be back!

With her stomach sated and the lounge chair cushion soft and squishy beneath her, Kate felt like taking a nap. Instead, she ruffled her hands through her short red hair ("scarlet," Gee had called it; but she'd liked it — especially once Neeve had assured her it would eventually wash out), and traced her new thin eyebrows with her fingertip. She'd run into Miss Munsfield in town yesterday, and Miss Munsfield hadn't recognized her at first when she'd said hello. "But Kate Callahan has chestnut hair," Miss Munsfield had said, putting on her glasses to peer intently at Kate's face. "And eyebrows," she'd added. Kate had laughed. At least the makeover had worked. But Miss Munsfield admonished her. "It looks just fine, but a woman shouldn't tart herself up too much. You're a beautiful girl, and there's no need to go parading around in outlandish hairstyles just to get people to notice you. You were just fine as you were."

Kate hadn't been trying to get noticed. That wasn't the goal (although it had been the result — the new red color and even the eyebrows had drawn lots of attention again at clinic). But Miss Munsfield's comment had made her want to spend some time reassessing her New Me list. Kate looked back at her handwriting in the book. Even though it was only about a week old, it seemed like she'd written it ages ago.

THE NEW ME
Makeover (get tan!)
Be braver
Get in shape
New interests
Pierce ears
Wear bikini

Kate felt like she couldn't really check anything off the list. The makeover was the closest to complete — her hair and eyebrows were done, and her teeth were definitely whiter (it seemed), but she still wasn't tan, and the expensive cellulite cream had done nothing (truth be told, she really wasn't sure what cellulite was, or what the cream was supposed to do for it). The bikini had only gotten her into trouble, and her ears were still bare. She allowed herself that she might be a tiny bit braver — since she'd asked for one or two donations with Hillary — and she was trying to get in shape by eating healthier. In fact, Kate picked up her pen and crossed out "Get in shape," replacing it with "Get healthy." There. She smiled down at the edited list. That was better.

But new interests. It was the one thing she'd done nothing about. Hmmm.

A black-and-yellow hornet droned by and then back-tracked, hovering to inspect Kate's pink sweater. She hated bees and was sure that she must be allergic. But instead of waving at it frantically, as she usually did, she tried Hillary's approach, and sat perfectly still. The hornet actually landed on her sleeve, and she sat motionless, paralyzed by fear, until the bee finally got bored and flew away. Kate was shaken but proud of herself. *Phew, that was close*, she thought.

The screen door squeaked and then banged closed gently. Kate looked up to see Gee waving at her, coming across the terrace with two iced teas in her hands.

"Mind if I join you?" called Gee.

Kate smiled. "Sure!"

Gee came and sat on the lounge chair next to Kate, handing her the iced tea. It was caramel brown, loaded with ice and lemon slices, and a chunk of freshly crushed mint floated on top. Gee always minted her tea, and Kate liked it like that, too.

Gee looked at Kate's notebook with interest, and Kate, following her glance, snapped it shut quickly.

"What are you working on?" asked Gee, swinging her legs up onto the lounge and reclining back. She cradled her glass in her hands.

"Nothing," said Kate. "Just some ideas."

"Recipes?" asked Gee hopefully.

"No."

"How's the needlepoint going?" Gee had taught Kate to needlepoint last year and it had become a passion they both shared. But Kate had been neglecting it lately. It was just so . . . slow, or time-consuming or something. She still liked it, but it was hard to fit it into her busy days.

Kate sighed. "I haven't had much time to work on it this week," she said.

"It is hard to find the time to slow down and do the things you love. Especially when you're surrounded by such fun cousins." Gee looked out over the lawn and down to the sound below.

"Yeah." And then, "I'm not so sure I love it anymore, Gee." She hadn't considered it until she'd said it aloud. Did she still love it? What *did* she still love? She hadn't been doing enough of the things she loved lately. She'd been embarrassed to take out her knitting, still smarting from Sloan's comments on the beach. She'd been excited to talk with Miss Munsfield, but she hadn't picked up a paintbrush since. Was she happier not doing those things? She'd written "New interests" on her list. But what could they be?

Gee turned her head and looked at her. "Are you okay, sweetheart?"

Kate wasn't sure. "I don't know. I'm just . . . I'm not sure . . . who I am, or what I'm supposed to be right now."

Gee nodded. "That happens. It means you're growing up."

"I guess. But I don't know what I'm turning into." Kate fingered her earlobe. It was hot and swollen, and there was some pus around the hole Sloan had made. She'd put peroxide on it, finally, at Phoebe's suggestion (she couldn't believe she hadn't thought of it sooner! All her years of playing nurse to everyone else, and she'd forgotten to take care of herself!). It seemed to help a little bit.

Gee turned on her side and put her glass down on the little white iron table next to her. She propped herself up on one elbow and looked carefully at Kate. "Throughout your whole life, there will be periods of change, some bigger than others. I remember a significant one from when I was about your age. I had a best friend who was *it*; the be-all and end-all. Everyone loved her — and she was so confident and trendy. She had all these older sisters who showed her how to dress and act and what music to listen to. I was just this gawky kid. I hadn't caught up yet. I didn't know how to talk to new people, or what to wear or say. I was so awkward. I remember it like it was yesterday. And I wanted so badly to be like her."

Kate looked at Gee with interest. It was hard to imagine her gawky or awkward. She was so graceful and beautiful. "So what did you do?" she asked.

"Well, at first, I tried to be like her: dressed like her, used her expressions, followed her interests. But it wasn't authentic. It didn't work, and people could tell I wasn't being myself. It was just artificial, and artifice scares people away because they feel unsure of you. So I gave that all up and I just hung around on the sidelines for a while and observed. I wasn't ready yet to make my debut," Gee chuckled. "But I picked up lots of ideas — things that worked and things that didn't. And in the meantime, I spent time on my own doing the things I really loved to do. Riding horses, drawing, even playing with my dollhouse, sometimes. And after a while, I was ready. I knew who I was and what I liked, and I think that one day, everything just clicked. I felt confident, and people sensed that. And you know, confidence draws boys like bees to honey." Gee laughed. "But much more importantly, it makes you feel good about yourself. Secure in yourself."

Kate thought of the hornet she'd just shooed away and smiled.

"So that's when you got confident?" she asked.

"In some ways, and for a while, yes. But there are many times in your life where your confidence wavers, and you need to shore yourself up again. I remember going away to boarding school, and the insecurity I felt there, with all those new girls — many of them more glamorous or sophisticated or smarter than I. Or at college, in the beginning. And even as a new wife, and then especially as a new mother. It's hard to change, whether it's from being a child into a teenager, or a wife into a mother."

"So what do you do to make it work?" Kate prodded. She was sitting up now, intrigued.

"Well, it's important to spend time with people who know and love you. That makes you feel secure. But it's just as important to make new friends. For one thing, they might be feeling some of what you're feeling in life, and that can be comforting. But also, when you see yourself through new eyes, and see how new friends respond to you, it gives you a stronger sense of the image you're projecting. You might be surprised to find that new people see you in a different way than the people who've known you forever."

Kate nodded, thinking of Lark and how surprised she'd been to discover that Lark thought she was cool and good at stuff, even though Lark had mostly seen her at her worst this summer. "What else?" she asked.

"I'd say that I think it's absolutely essential to focus on doing the things you love, the things you're good at — even if your friends aren't interested in those things — to give yourself a sense of accomplishment, and the joy of doing them, as well. Happiness is contagious, and people respond positively to it. So is passion. You don't even need to be good at something, but if you love doing it, and do it often, you'll gain confidence in yourself and your talents. People are very attracted to that, and their reaction to you can give you even more confidence. It just builds that way."

Like singing, thought Kate. *Or cooking.* "Hmmm," she said. "I've been feeling like I need some new interests," she confessed.

Gee's eyes widened in surprise. "Whatever for? You have wonderful interests. And you're very good at them."

"It's just that lately I've realized they're so . . ." Kate searched for a replacement term, not wanting to offend Gee. But she gave up. ". . . old-ladyish. Sorry." She smiled guiltily.

Gee pretended to be offended. "Do you think of me as an old lady?!" But she smiled. "I don't think your interests are old-ladyish at all, if I do say so myself. I think they're . . . timeless. And traditional. Classic. You're not a trend-chaser. You know what you like and who you are."

"I don't see it that way," said Kate, shaking her head.

"Well, you used to. Not that long ago," said Gee softly.

"I guess." Kate thought about that for a minute. She had seen it that way, up until this summer. But the cousins had made her feel out of it, with Hillary's outdoorsy energy and Neeve's trendiness and Phoebe's intellectual vigor. Should she change? Or not?

Gee watched her. "You know, you don't have to grow up all at once," she said finally. "I didn't."

Kate smiled.

"In fact, I still haven't grown up," Gee laughed.

They were quiet for a moment as Kate absorbed this idea. Her list had seemed so important. So necessary. But, did she have to change? Was she already changed enough? It was so confusing. She picked up her notebook, and flipped to the list page. She reread it and then closed the book, while Gee watched.

"Just a little shopping list," fibbed Kate, not able to look Gee in the eye. "Stuff I don't really need."

"I see," said Gee. Kate couldn't see it, but a small smile played at her lips.

They sat in companionable silence for a moment. And then Kate spoke.

"Knitting is cool, isn't it, Gee?"

"Very," answered Gee wisely.

They were quiet again, and then Gee said, "Sweetheart, what happened to your ear?"

Kate's hand flew to her lobe. "Oh? This? Um." She fingered it gingerly. "I . . . I let Sloan try to pierce my ear." There, she'd admitted it. She'd been trying to hide it from Gee for days, and then had finally decided that it wasn't that noticeable.

"Let me see," said Gee, lifting her reading glasses to her eyes. "Ouch. That looks like it hurts."

Kate nodded. It did.

"Where did this all take place?" Gee asked.

Oh dear. Kate remembered Gee saying they should avoid Sloan for a while. No visiting. She'd conveniently put that out of her mind when she'd gone to Sloan's house.

"At Sloan's," she confessed.

Gee set her mouth in a grim line. "Not a good idea, as we discussed. Nothing good ever happens when Sloan is around."

"I know, Gee. I'm sorry. It's just that I was . . . desperate."

"Desperate for what?" asked Gee.

"To get my ears pierced. To be . . . cool." It sounded silly when she said it out loud, especially to Gee.

"I see," said Gee. Then she sighed. "I think we'd better take you over to the clinic tomorrow to let someone take a look at it."

Kate braced herself, waiting for a lecture about disobeying

Gee, but nothing more came. Gee seemed to see that Kate felt bad enough as it was.

"Okay," said Kate. It would be a relief to heal this thing up. It was starting to gross her out.

"I'll call for an appointment," said Gee.

"Thanks," said Kate, and she stood and scurried down to the Dorm before Gee could say anything else.

CHAPTER EIGHTEEN

The Clinic

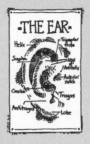

Kate slept restlessly that night, and she was overtired and a bit out of sorts the next morning. She was glad that she got to miss sailing clinic because of her appointment, but she felt a little lonely as she sat in the kitchen and the others rode away, waving solemnly as if they were leaving forever.

At quarter of nine, Gee returned to the kitchen, showered and dressed impeccably, as usual. She grabbed her car keys and her purse off the counter. "Ready?" she asked brightly. Her trademark pink lipstick was in place, and she looked ready to take on the world.

"Ready!" said Kate, tentatively touching her ear. Ouch.

They rode to the clinic, speaking of nothing much, and were soon ensconced in the waiting room with its freezing air-conditioning, plastic chairs, and back issues of *People* magazine. Kate had brought her knitting, and she was just pulling it out of the bag when her name was called. She stuffed it back in.

"Kate Callahan?" A woman poked her head into the room with a clipboard in her hand, and Kate and Gee rose to follow her to the examining room.

Once inside, the woman introduced herself, then proceeded to ask all sorts of questions about the ear-piercing incident, including what sorts of "instruments" Kate's friend had used, and things like that, making notes on the fresh page of Kate's chart.

"I'll get the nurse for you now," the woman said, and she ducked out.

Kate had thought she was the nurse. She looked at Gee, and then there was a quiet knock on the door, and who walked in but Sloan's mother! Mrs. Bicket! Kate nearly gasped aloud in her surprise. It had never crossed her mind that Sloan's mother would be the one to see her!

"Good morning!" said Mrs. Bicket. "Hello, Samantha, hello, Kate." She looked down at Kate's chart and then sat in the swivel chair next to the counter so she could make notes in the chart while they exchanged pleasantries. Kate was shocked. She looked at Gee. Had *Gee* known that they'd be seeing Sloan's *mom?* All the things she knew about the Bickets and their relationship with the Callahans came flooding into her mind. Rivalry. Competition. And the things Sloan had said about her mother. Kate couldn't believe Gee was being so friendly. But that was just Gee. She always maintained that you had to try to stay friendly with people when you lived on an island.

And then Mrs. Bicket said, "Samantha, do you mind if Kate and I spend a few minutes alone?"

Gee seemed a little surprised, but she rose and gave Kate a kiss on the head. "Of course." Then she left the room, shutting the door behind her.

Mrs. Bicket turned back to Kate. "Body piercing by a nonprofessional is dangerous, and especially for someone your age. I hate to see kids treating their bodies recklessly like this." Her mouth was set in a grim line. "How did this little injury occur, if you don't mind my asking?" asked Mrs. Bicket.

Kate's thumb flew to her mouth and she bit the nail. For an instant, she debated lying, but she quickly realized that lying might make the situation worse.

"Uh, Sloan did it for me," she said finally.

Mrs. Bicket's eyes widened, and she exhaled a little breath of surprise. "How did that come about?"

Kate explained about Sloan's offering to pierce her ear that day on the beach, and how she had been turned down at Gullboutique; she tried as hard as possible to portray Sloan as a friend helping out a friend in need. Mrs. Bicket shook her head as she took notes.

"I am so sorry," she said, looking up at Kate. "Sloan should know better than that. It was very dangerous and unsanitary, what she did. I'm going to have a word with her when I get home."

"No! Please don't!" Kate would die if she'd gotten Sloan in trouble, and not just because Sloan would make her life a living hell. It was mostly because Sloan had been so nice to her that day: offering to help her, and then opening up about her problems with her mother. "What about . . . doctor-patient confidentiality?" asked Kate, desperately.

Mrs. Bicket looked at her closely, and then smiled. She sighed. "Alright. I guess you're right. Just don't, I repeat, don't let someone do this to you again. I'll figure out a way to discuss it with Sloan, too, without letting on that you told me."

Kate smiled weakly in relief. Phew.

Mrs. Bicket stood to examine Kate's ear under a bright light, gently squeezing it between her thumb and forefinger. While she did, she asked Kate about her summer, and what she'd been doing. For some reason, Kate found Mrs. Bicket easy to talk to, and she mentioned her hobbies: cooking, decorating, knitting. And then she noticed a small smile playing on Mrs. Bicket's lips.

"What?" asked Kate with a smile of her own.

Mrs. Bicket waved her hand. "Nothing. I've just been wondering where Sloan's new fascination with knitting had come from. She's after me to help her get yarn and needles and learn how to do it."

Kate's heart surged in unexpected triumph and she laughed aloud. *Aha! So Sloan didn't think knitting was for losers after all!* Then she remembered Sloan's comment about how her mom never had time for her, and she sobered immediately. She looked at

Mrs. Bicket carefully, summoning up her courage, and then she said, "You should. Do it together. That's how I started. My mom and I used to do it together. We even took classes, and it was fun."

Mrs. Bicket held her gaze for a second, and then a bemused smile lit up her face. "You're right. I should." Kate looked back at her encouragingly, and Mrs. Bicket sighed. "I will."

Kate smiled. Sloan would be psyched, and Kate was kind of shocked to realize that she felt happy for Sloan, as if Sloan were just any other friend.

Mrs. Bicket wrote out two prescriptions: one for an antibiotic pill for Kate to take for five days, and one for a really strong ointment that Kate was to put on her ear three times a day, both sides for a week. She promised these two things would clear up the infection by the end of the week, and that Kate would probably not have a scar, seeing as how the needle hadn't been through her ear for long enough for scar tissue to form around it. She mentioned that the antibiotic would make Kate more sensitive to the sun, and said that Kate should avoid prolonged exposure and use loads of sunscreen so she didn't burn. She added, "But I guess with that gorgeous skin of yours, you're already sensible about the sun." Then she patted Kate on the head, offered her a lollipop in a joking way that showed she knew Kate was too old for such things, and prepared to leave. But as she put her hand on the door, she asked, "What made you willing to let Sloan pierce your ear, if you don't mind my asking?"

"Oh. Um." She decided to confess, no matter how silly it sounded, and no matter whose mother she was talking to. "Uh . . . I wanted to be cool." Mrs. Bicket didn't flinch. She's probably heard it all before, realized Kate. "I wanted to be cool, and it seemed like getting my ears pierced was one way to begin."

Mrs. Bicket was quiet for a moment, and then she shook her head. "So much talk about coolness. In my own home, too, of course." She smiled sadly and shook her head. "She's cool, he's cool, I'm uncool, how can I be cooler?" Mrs. Bicket gave a little laugh. "It is so hard being a kid, isn't it?"

Kate nodded, but inside she was wondering if it was Sloan Mrs. Bicket was talking about. Could it be possible that Sloan ever thought herself uncool? Nah.

"Um, Mrs. Bicket? Remember, you won't say anything to Sloan about this, right?"

Mrs. Bicket was solemn. "I promise. And anyway, I do know that Sloan thinks the world of you. It's 'Kate this' and 'the Callahan cousins that.'" She shook her head with a weary smile. "She's had a lot of fun with you all visiting this summer."

Kate's smile froze on her face. Sloan talked about them? To her *mom*? As if they were her *friends*? Weird! Maybe her mom was just exaggerating to make Kate feel good? But she seemed sincere. Kate thought back to all the looks she'd caught on Sloan's face in the past week or so; looks of yearning, of envy, of sadness. Kate was known for her sensitivity, so she knew she wasn't just imagining them. They were real.

"Bye, sweetie. Feel better!" Mrs. Bicket shut the door, and Kate stared blindly at the poster with the diagram of the inner ear that hung on the wall of the examining room. *Wonders never cease,* she told herself. And then, *I've got to talk to the others.*

Later that afternoon, the girls were on the trampoline. Neeve and Hillary were practicing their back flips, and Kate was quoting statistics about trampoline-related injuries that she'd read in one of her mom's magazines back home. Phoebe had jumped a bit, then climbed down to read her book, which was, as she said, at the "best part."

"You always say that!" protested Neeve, her denim skirt inflating like a bell in the breeze each time she sailed down from a jump.

"Well, I read a lot. There's always a best part."

Kate had been thinking about Mrs. Bicket all day. And Sloan. The others had freaked out when they came home from clinic and she told them who she'd seen. They wanted to know if she was nice to Kate, and if they'd discussed Sloan. Kate told them she had been nice, and that no, they hadn't discussed Sloan. Doctor-patient confidentiality works both ways, she'd reasoned, feeling a little guilty for protecting Sloan.

Now she finally formed the idea that had been growing in her mind. She summoned up her courage, and said, "Guys? I think we need to let Sloan win."

Neeve and Hillary stopped jumping, and Phoebe's eyes darted away from her book, looking searchingly at Kate. *Must not be that good of a best part,* thought Kate.

"What are you talking about?" asked Neeve in disbelief.

"After we've come so far?" added Hillary.

"No way," said Phoebe. "I'm not throwing in the towel for that little jerk!"

"I think we need to," continued Kate.

"You're just trying to get her to be your friend," said Phoebe, eyes blazing now. "You just want to suck up to her or something. Why would you just hand victory to her on a silver platter like that?"

Kate wouldn't take the bait. She was in no mood for a fight. "Because I think she needs it," she said simply.

That stunned the others into silence. They considered this for a minute. It was hard, Kate knew, to readjust your concept of the enemy. To see her as a living, breathing person with her own hopes and fears. But this summer had given them glimpses of Sloan's softer side.

"Why are you acting so mature and charitable toward her all of a sudden?" demanded Phoebe.

Kate remained calm. "You know, I've seen a lot of her lately — sides of her that I didn't know existed. And I think she's jealous of us. And I think she actually wants to be our friend."

There was a pause, and then Neeve said quietly, "I've seen that look in her eyes myself."

Another pause, and then Hillary said, "Me too."

Kate smiled gratefully at them.

"Come on, you two! Don't just roll over and play dead like that!" Phoebe was enraged. "We need to beat her."

"Listen, Phoebe. When the summer's over, and we all go back to our own lives, Sloan will still be here. This is her home. I just think it's mean for us to come in and try to take everything away from her." Kate was kind of making it up as she went along, but it was all true, she realized, as she said it.

"Yeah," agreed Neeve.

"And I was thinking, maybe there's something else we could do to help Gee with the benefit. I mean, the party is going to be here, after all. Maybe we could, like, help out around the house, or do party bags, or whatever."

Phoebe narrowed her eyes and looked at Kate. "I think this is all because you want to get out of having to ask for more donations."

"Phoebe!" said Neeve. "That's mean!"

Kate shrugged. "Maybe."

But Hillary jumped in. "Bee, if you'd seen Kate the other day, you'd know that's not true anymore. She got really good at it in the end. Especially once she started talking to people who shared her interests." Hillary smiled at Kate. "Painting, flowers, *candy* . . ."

"Interests," scoffed Phoebe. "All that homemaking stuff! That stuff isn't real. It's all just . . . disposable. Replaceable. Edible. It doesn't last."

"Sweaters last," said Neeve.

"You know what I mean," said Phoebe. "It's not important. It's just clutter."

"Phoebe!" Hillary was aghast. "I suppose what you do — all that reading and research — that's all meaningful?"

"Of course. It *improves* me," sniffed Phoebe. "Not that anyone would ever think to ask me about it."

"We ask you all the time about what you're reading!" protested Hillary. "It's just that it's always way above our heads, so we can't exactly discuss it with you."

"Kate doesn't ask," said Phoebe indignantly.

"So what?" said Neeve. "Why do you care?"

There was a pause. And then Phoebe said in a small voice. "I care because I'm the only one that Kate never asked for help."

"What?" Kate was stunned. "What are you talking about?"

Phoebe drew herself up and lifted her chin in the air. "You've asked the others for their help in making yourself over, but you never asked me."

"Of course I did," said Kate. "I asked for your help right in the beginning!" She couldn't believe what Phoebe was saying. It was so unlike her to care about this kind of petty stuff. Wasn't it?

"Well, to be exact, you said in the beginning that you wanted me to help you find new interests. But then you never came back to me. You just continued on with all of those things you do, and you never asked me again."

Kate was incredulous. "And you're offended by that?"

Phoebe reached up to redo the bun in her hair. "Well, yes. I am. Obviously you don't think I have anything to offer. I mean, certainly I don't bake delicious things to hand out to all of my friends, nor do I hand-make beautiful creations for my loved ones. But I have excellent interests, too, you know."

This was the closest Kate had ever seen Phoebe come to crying. And it was her fault! She couldn't believe it! She jumped off the side of the trampoline where she'd been spotting the others so they didn't fall off. Then she sat next to Phoebe and engulfed her in a hug. Phoebe remained stiff — self-contained and un-touchy-feely as ever — so after a minute Kate pulled away.

"I am so sorry, Bee! I didn't even realize what I did! I didn't mean to make you feel bad. I swear!" She looked at the others for help, but they were too stunned by Phoebe's unusual outburst.

"Listen," continued Kate. "I'd never in a million years mean to hurt you. And the truth is, I just never quite got to that part on my list. Because at first, I thought all of my interests were lame, but then I finally decided that, for me, they were actually pretty good. And I enjoy them. So that's why I never came back, hounding you for help, like I did the others."

"That's fine," said Phoebe. "I'm not hurt." But she clearly was.

Kate sighed. "You know, the truth is, I've also been kind of mad at you. You've been picking on me so much lately that I've been kind of avoiding you —"

Phoebe started to protest, but Kate continued.

"I know you think it's just teasing, the whole 'You couldn't stick up for a flea,' and 'You're an old lady,' and all that stuff. But it hurts my feelings. A lot. And I'm tired of it. It makes me not want to be around you. I know it all started as jokes, and you're so witty and all that, but it's started to make me feel terrible."

Phoebe was quiet for a minute now. She flipped the pages of her book quickly, creating a little breeze. "I guess you're right. I've gotten a little too mean-spirited lately. At first it was because you're so . . . you were such a chicken about things. Finding the island, and boats, and going up the hill in the dark. So I wanted to set myself apart from you. I didn't want to be dragged down by you, because I, I have chicken tendencies, too, and I didn't want to let that side of me win. It would be too easy and also, then my summer wouldn't be as fun. And then it just kind of grew into . . . just," she looked up at Kate, and her voice turned stern and accusatory. "What the heck is going on with you? And why do you want to hang around Sloan? And what's up with all this 'cool' talk all the time? That's not what you're like!"

"Why do you care, though?" asked Kate fervently.

Phoebe threw down her book in a most un-Phoebe-like way, causing Kate to draw in her breath sharply. Phoebe reached up to redo her bun. "I care because . . . I hate to see you giving in to someone like Sloan. It's so immature. And you're so much better than her! I know you think she's so great, but she really isn't. And it drives me crazy that that's the kind of girl you look up to; someone so . . . unworthy! It's just like back home. . . ."

Phoebe stopped, and her eyes welled with tears. The others didn't know what to say, they were so stunned by Phoebe's sudden outburst. But finally Kate found her voice.

"What happened back home?" asked Kate.

Phoebe waved her hand impatiently in the air, brushing away the question. She clenched her jaw and knit her white eyebrows together, then she looked up at the sky to get the tears to drain back into her tear ducts. She exhaled through her mouth and looked back at Kate.

"My class got ruined last year by a queen bee."

Kate looked at her in confusion. "What?"

"You know, one of those girls who has to take charge of the class and pit everyone against each other, creating infighting and cliques, all the while prioritizing trendiness and other useless and meritless value systems."

"Oh." For once, Kate actually understood what Phoebe was talking about when she used big words. The same thing had happened in the grade above Kate back home, two years ago. Kate had watched in horror, from a distance, glad that she wasn't a part of it. She knew parents had been called in, and there had been homeroom transfers — which was the first time that had ever been allowed to happen midyear at her school. Anyway, it had been really bad, so she had an inkling of what Phoebe must've gone through.

She looked at Phoebe closely, and asked in a soft voice: "Were you one of the, um . . . ?"

"Losers?" spat Phoebe. "The wanna-bes? The outcasts? Yes, as a matter of fact, I was. And people who had been my best friends suddenly were evading me and not returning my calls and making plans without me for Saturday nights, just so they could be with the cool girls." Tears filled her eyes again.

Neeve and Hillary had been quiet for a bit. Now Neeve spoke up. "So how did you leave it, then? What happened at the end of the year?"

Phoebe composed herself again and said, "Well . . ." She cleared her throat, dislodging the frog. "Well, my '*best* friend,' or the person who had been my best friend since preschool and who had completely ditched me, she and I kind of made up, but that was really only because she got dumped. And my mom was going to put in a request to make sure I wasn't in the same homeroom as that . . . *Amanda* . . . next year. If I am, then I won't go to school. I'll just home-school myself."

Hillary smiled. "But you love school, Bee!"

Phoebe's eyes flashed. "That's what made me so mad. Amanda ruined it for me! I dreaded going! I had stomachaches every morning! I skipped school — staying home sick — just to avoid her when I couldn't take it anymore. She ruined school for me last year." Phoebe turned to Kate. "Just like Sloan has the potential to ruin Gull for all of us."

Kate was thoughtful for a moment. "I don't think there's any chance of that happening, Bee. For real. I mean, I'm onto her now. I think she's just a lonely, insecure girl whose mom doesn't spend enough time with her. . . ."

". . . who is bored by living on this tiny island," interrupted Neeve.

"And doesn't know how to play nicely with others," added Hillary with a grin.

Kate nodded. "And anyway, she doesn't have any power over us at all. We have each other, and we're related, and she can't change that! We're cousins, Bee!"

"Cousins forever!" said Neeve brightly.

Kate smiled and continued. "I know I've made a couple of bad choices lately, but in the end, I'd always choose you guys over Sloan. And anyway, at the end of the summer, we get to leave, and Sloan has to stay here, with no real friends. It's sad."

Phoebe was softening, Kate could tell. She pressed on to seal the deal. "So listen, let's let Sloan win, okay? And we can know inside that we're the real winners, because we have each other."

"Oh please, that's so hokey, Kate!" cried Neeve, making Phoebe laugh.

"But it's true!" Things were beginning to seem normal again, but before Kate let Phoebe jump on the bandwagon and start ragging on her, she added, "Please be nice to me, Bee. I need a break from the teasing for a while, okay?"

Phoebe bit her lip and nodded. "I'm sorry. I guess I've been no better than a Sloan or an Amanda."

Kate gave her a squeeze, which Phoebe received stiffly, as usual. "Yes, you have. Way better. Now, about those interests. I need some help researching healthy food and recipes down at the library. And also some new sweater patterns. Would you help me locate some stuff?"

"Sure. I'd be more than glad to," offered Phoebe, calmer now. "And Kate?" She reached over and patted Kate awkwardly on the knee. "I'm sorry."

"I know," said Kate, putting her hand over Phoebe's.

They were quiet for a minute, all of them. "So how about the Sloan thing, guys? What do you say?" prodded Kate. "Will you do it? For me, if not for her?"

And one by one, they all nodded.

CHAPTER NINETEEN
The Dive from the Dock

By Thursday, the party preparations were well under way at
The Sound. The tent men had come on Wednesday to erect
an enormous white tent over a level section of Gee's side yard,
and the girls had an amazing time watching the process of
hammering in poles, and tying ropes, and then the grand fi-
nale of the tent being hoisted into position. Every day new
deliveries were arriving at the house, and Sheila and Gee were
like chickens with their heads cut off, trying to organize it
all: rental tables, chairs, hurricane lanterns for the tables, a
portable toilet truck with individual bathrooms of unlikely
beauty inside, a platform for the band and a dance floor, cases
of glasses and liquor. It was fun having all the activity be at
their house, and the girls were consequently spending more
time at home. Lark had become somewhat of a permanent
fixture too, and although her omnipresence annoyed Kate at
first, after a while she got used to her and began to appreciate

Lark's dry, quiet sense of humor and her helpfulness, as well as her general enthusiasm for life and especially all things Callahan.

In trying to reinvent herself, Kate had condemned Lark's enthusiasm at first, finding it desperate the way Lark revealed her true feelings, mainly because deep down inside, she knew that she had a tendency to do the same herself. (Kate's mother had once told her that the things that bother us most about other people are the things that drive us crazy in ourselves, and Kate knew this was the case with Lark.) But genuine enthusiasm and energy were so much more preferable to Sloan's snottiness or condemnation of everything. Thinking back to that day on the beach with Sloan, Kate realized that Sloan was just trying to feel her way through life like anyone else; she threw things out there like "Knitting is uncool" because it was easier to just criticize *everything* and do *nothing* than it was to try something and potentially be thought a fool (even if the chances of that were slim). Kate came to the decision that if someone criticized something without providing a good alternative, then she was just paranoid: too afraid to let herself go and have fun. And Kate didn't want to be like that.

Thursday afternoon, the girls sat in the kitchen to review their donations. Lark had, of course, come over after clinic and joined them for a picnic lunch out at the Promised Land, the cute private cove where the girls had learned to swim as little kids. Tomorrow, the benefit committee would be reviewing all of the donations and printing up the catalogs for the auction and raffle, so after lunch, the girls began to get everything in order.

Phoebe was making a list in their notebook as they went around the table and told what they had gotten. Among other things were a telescope from Lark's dad; a fishing expedition that Neeve had gotten from Talbot and his dad, a commercial fisherman; Hillary had gotten Mr. Booker to give a full outfit of sailing gear; Phoebe had gotten the island newspaper to donate a subscription and a free birthday ad, and had gotten Mrs. Merrihew at the library to donate twelve hours of ancestry research. They were quite proud of themselves, because combined with all the other stuff it came to a lot. No one had mentioned how Kate had convinced them to bow out at the end; they'd just known to keep it a secret. And Kate, for one, was incredibly relieved that the solicitation process was now over. She'd gotten decent at it, even though she needed a partner. But she didn't want to do it anymore — and certainly never alone.

They were just wrapping up their review of the list when Gee came rushing in from a last-minute benefit committee meeting and asked if they'd be willing to help stuff party bags for the event. All of the other committee members were busy, and it needed to get done; Gee offered them a trip to The Dip in exchange for their work, but of course she didn't need to bribe them. Lark volunteered to stay, too, and Gee said why didn't she just stay for dinner, then Hillary asked her to sleep over, and everything was ducky, until Lark realized she'd promised Sloan that she'd spend the night at her house.

"Maybe Sloan could come help and, uh, sleep over, too?" offered Kate.

Lark looked around the table; she knew how much Phoebe and the others disliked Sloan, but Phoebe was feeling a tiny bit more sympathetic toward Sloan after the cousins' chat on the trampoline. So she shrugged and said, "I guess, since it's for a good cause. We just need to ask Gee because Sloan is banned from our house."

Lark's eyes widened, but Hillary interrupted, saying, "She's not 'banned,' Phoebe. Gee just said we always get into trouble when Sloan comes over, so we shouldn't ask her for a while."

"Huh." Phoebe snorted and folded her arms. "We still need to ask."

They sought out Gee in the kitchen, and she agreed that Sloan could be invited over to help, but thought that a sleep-over was a bit much. "I'll drive Sloan home when you're finished, but let's make it a reasonable hour, shall we?" And the girls agreed, and Lark went off to make the call. Kate was a little nervous having Sloan to her house again, since she was unsure where things stood between them. Were they friends or not? And how would Phoebe and the others behave once Sloan was actually here?

She didn't have much time to think it over, since Sloan arrived almost instantly, and she'd brought her donation coupons to turn in to Gee, as Lark had instructed on the phone. In spite of themselves, the girls oohed and ahhed over what she'd gotten, and she smirked in pride, pleased with the attention and accolades.

Gee laid out all of the party bag supplies in the living room, and after dinner, the girls created an assembly line. Each little paper shopping bag had to be stickered with a label that said the clinic's name on it, and then each bag needed to get a flyer about the clinic, a bottle of perfume called Privet, a gull-shaped key chain, a small bottle of wine, and a "Caroline & Thomas Sheehan Health Clinic" t-shirt. Neeve brought Hillary's iPod up from the Dorm and cranked up the tunes, and the music and the many hands made the work go faster than they would have thought, even though they stuffed five hundred bags!

By the time they were finished, it had grown stuffy in the living room, and everyone needed a little fresh air. So Sheila gave them a big bowl of fresh fruit salad (she was being very supportive of Kate's search for healthy snacks), and along with some little plates and forks they took it down to the bathing pavilion to sit at the table and eat. It was dark out, but there was an overhead light in the shape of a Chinese lantern that hung from the peaked roof of the small structure, so the girls could chat and see each other.

The talk quickly turned to boys and who everyone thought was cute. Neeve admitted that she had a crush on Talbot, but felt that they were better as friends, and she didn't want to mess that up. Lark liked Atticus, and Hillary had spotted a counselor in training at clinic whom she had her eye on. Phoebe passed, and said she thought that Jeremy Adams, a guy from her English class at home, was really the one for her. Kate mentioned a friend of Ned's from boarding school. After talking with Sloan on the beach that day, she'd been thinking about him a lot. And then it was Sloan's turn.

Sloan loved the spotlight, and she drew out the cat-and-mouse game of the others begging her to tell them and her refusing. Finally, she sensed that her audience was losing interest and ready to move on, and she grabbed their attention back like a master conductor. "Okay, you wore me down," she announced. "It's Mark."

"Who?" None of the Callahans knew who he was. Except maybe for Kate.

"Is that the one at mini-golf that night?" Kate asked knowing that her asking was a full acknowledgement of the fact that she'd been watching Sloan that night, and also that Sloan had not said hello to the Callahans.

"Yes," said Sloan, ducking her head in a pantomime of shyness that she clearly didn't feel.

"Is he the one who works at Coolidge's?" asked Kate.

"Yes!" said Sloan in surprise. "How did you know?"

"Oh, because on the beach you said the older teenage guys who were meeting you worked at Coolidge's, and then you said one of them was named Mark and he had black hair, and then I saw you with the black-haired guy at . . ." Sloan's eyes were widening with every word and Kate stopped herself. She felt like Lark: she had revealed that she had paid attention to every morsel of information that Sloan had told her, not to mention remembering it and then spending the time to put the information all together. It sounded kind of dorky, now that she was regurgitating it. There was nothing more uncool than someone who remembered too much about other people's business.

And yet, Sloan seemed pleased after, and began acting all buddy-buddy with Kate, directing her Mark stories to her and even implying that Kate knew him ("Oh, you know Mark. Or, you know who he is . . . ," she'd say conspiratorially, and Kate would wince in embarrassment at having revealed herself). Phoebe kept rolling her eyes, and after a while, took it upon herself to ask Sloan just how old this "older teenage guy" was. There was a long pause before Sloan had admitted that he was thirteen, and Phoebe had sat back with a smirk, satisfied that she'd put Sloan in her place. After all, he was less than a year older than them.

A breeze picked up, and Kate ran to grab sweaters for everyone from the Dorm. When she returned she noticed Sloan admiring the one she'd selected for her, and searching for its label.

"Oh, I made that one," said Kate dismissively. "There's no label."

Sloan was flabbergasted. "You *made* this?"

"Yeah."

"Like, as in, knit it?"

"Uh-huh. It's not very good, I know. It was one of the first ones I ever made. That's why I had to keep it for myself. Usually I . . ."

"I can't believe it!" said Sloan. "You should . . . you should, like, go into business or something!"

Kate smiled. "Yeah, right."

"I'm serious. This is so good, and you even think it's not your best work."

Sloan had let her guard down and was showing genuine enthusiasm for once, without any self-consciousness. *See, this is when she's actually likeable,* thought Kate. *When she's being herself and not busy trying to be cool.*

"Hey! You know what?" asked Sloan. "You should donate a custom-made sweater to the raffle! Like, the person can pick out the style, within reason, and the yarn, and then you knit it for them. How amazing would that be?"

Kate was flattered and wished she'd thought of it herself. "Good idea! I'll add it to the list. I'm much better at knitting now than I was when I made that."

And then Gee came walking down the hill, her pale green cardigan pulled tightly around her. "Ooh, it's chilly out here tonight. I hope it's not like this on Saturday for the party! We'd have to bring down blankets from the linen closet!"

The girls laughed and invited Gee to join them, but she demurred, saying it was time for bed. "Thank you all so much for your help tonight, and with all of the wonderful things you got for the raffle and the auction. I hate to say it, but you got much better things than Mrs. Bennett usually gets. There are quite a few things I even have my eye on . . . like those rainbow pashminas from Gullboutique. I could use one right now!"

Kate and Sloan exchanged a smile, and then Gee said, "Sloan, dear, can I offer you a ride home? I hate to think of you biking all that way alone in the dark."

Sloan looked surprised for a moment, as if she'd forgotten that she, too, wasn't spending the night.

"Oh, no, Mrs. Callahan, I'm fine. I ride my bike all over in the dark."

Gee looked skeptical, but she said, "Okay, then. Well, I'll give your mother a call to let her know you're on your way. . . ."

"No!" Sloan looked alarmed, and then embarrassed that she's protested so vehemently. "No. She's working late tonight anyway, so I'll just go and then I'll be home by the time she gets in."

"If you say so. . . . Then, I think it's time for you girls to retire for the night. Say your goodbyes, and head off to bed. We've got a big weekend coming up, and it just wouldn't do for you girls to be overtired for it."

She walked back up the hill, and the six girls looked at one another.

"I am tired, actually," admitted Kate. So much had been going on, and it had taken a lot out of her.

Everyone stood, and Neeve went to turn out the pavilion light from up in the main house. They walked to the edge of the driveway to say goodnight to Sloan and see her off, but

Sloan seemed to just keep chatting as they stood there, despite their increasingly obvious hints that they were ready for bed.

Finally, Sloan said, "Who wants to go swimming?"

Kate was shocked awake. "Swimming? *Now?* It's freezing! And it's late. It's bedtime!"

But before anyone could stop her, Sloan was charging back down the yard, and past the swimming pool, even, until she'd reached the bathing pavilion. The girls hurried along behind her, despite their misgivings, trying to call her without attracting Gee's notice. At the pavilion, she yanked off her clothes until she was wearing just a bathing suit that she must've had on all along, underneath.

"Come on!" she cried quietly. "Are you all chicken?"

No one moved. She stood there with her hands on her hips, and Kate wondered what had gotten into her.

Phoebe said, "Sloan, Gee said it's time for you to go home. Isn't your mother going to be worried about you?"

"Actually, I told her I was sleeping here," Sloan said brashly.

The others exchanged glances. "Uh, why?" asked Hillary.

Neeve returned from the main house and joined them. "What's going on?"

"Sloan's going swimming," said Lark with wide eyes.

"Now?"

"Uh-huh."

"Come on, guys!" Sloan was shivering now in the breeze, and she looked so pathetic, and alone, and kind of desperate, that Kate felt a surge of pity for her. Clearly Sloan didn't want to go home, for whatever reason, and now she was trying to engage the rest of them in an activity that would keep her there for a while. Maybe she just didn't want to go home when her mom wasn't there. Maybe it was too lonely. Or maybe she felt really left out and wanted to stay with the rest of them. It was kind of sad that she had to go.

"I'll swim in the pool with you, if you want," offered Kate rashly, mostly to make Sloan feel better. What would a little dip before bedtime hurt if it made Sloan feel better?

But Sloan brushed her off. "Nah. Pools are for wimps. Wouldn't it be fun to jump off the railing here and into the sound? It'd make a great story."

Phoebe was disgusted. "Whatever. I'm going to bed," and she turned and left, heading off toward the Dorm.

"Me too," agreed Neeve and Hillary, and they, along with Lark, set off after Phoebe.

Which left Kate alone with Sloan on the dock. "Come on, Sloan. Why don't you put your clothes on and we could see if Gee could drive you home." It was true what Gee had said last week about bad things happening when Sloan came over. This was just downright weird, and about to turn bad if Kate couldn't talk Sloan into leaving.

"I'm going in. If you want to be a loser, you can stay right there. But if you want to be cool, you can come in with me," said Sloan defiantly, and with a flourish, she climbed up onto the railing and jumped, slicing into the dark water below with barely a splash.

CHAPTER TWENTY

Uncool

Kate gasped when Sloan disappeared. "Sloan!" she called, and she hurried to look over the edge. It was so dark that she could barely see anything. But then she heard a groan.

"Sloan?" she called frantically. "Sloan?"

"Here . . . ," said a pathetic voice. "I'm . . . I think I'm hurt . . . ," said Sloan. "Help."

Oh dear. Kate looked around for something to toss to Sloan. There was nothing.

"Hang on, Sloan, I'm going to get the others." She turned to run to the Dorm, but Sloan cried out.

"Wait! Don't leave me here alone! What if a shark comes? I think I'm bleeding!"

Double oh dear! "Sloan! Just . . ." Oh darn it. Kate was going to have to go in after her. There was nothing else to be done.

Quickly, she peeled off her clothes down to her underpants and t-shirt, and with a whispered "God help me!" she climbed over the railing and lowered herself gently down the ladder and into the water.

The shock of the cold water and the reality of swimming in the dark nearly knocked the wind out of her. "Aaah!" she yelled. "Sloan? Where are you? Swim over here right now! I'm not going any further!" She was in the water now, but she couldn't let go of the ladder, and her knees were trembling and her teeth were chattering in fear and cold.

"I can't. . . . Come get me," pleaded Sloan.

Oh for heaven's sake! "Where are you?"

"Over here."

Kate followed the sound of her voice, terror coursing through her veins and quickly warming her. She dog-paddled nervously in the direction of Sloan's voice, and whined in terror when a piece of seaweed (an imagined shark) brushed by her leg.

"Sloan, come on. This isn't funny. Where are you? I'm freezing!"

"Here . . . ," groaned Sloan.

Kate swam a little farther and groped blindly in the darkness. Finally, she felt someone. "Sloan?" she demanded in a high panicky voice.

"Uhh." It was she.

"Come on, Sloan. Take my hand and I'll pull you."

"I can't. I'm too scared."

Scared to get out of the water? This was getting ridiculous. *It's one thing to be scared to go in, but come on,* thought Kate. *I'm dying to get out, and* I'm *the scaredy-cat.*

"Sloan, you've got to help me or I can't help you." Kate was running out of energy, and suddenly all of her life-saving class instructions came flooding back to her. She'd had to take the class last year in school as part of her Phys Ed requirement. It was actually called "drown-proofing," and the name alone had terrified her. The lifeguards who taught the class made them do drills like tread water for a half hour fully dressed (with sneakers on) and their arms or legs tied together, or dive down and touch the bottom of the diving pool (14 feet), and then — the most insane and irrelevant thing — front and back somer-saults executed in the middle of the pool with no wall to push off. Kate had been traumatized but had absorbed every morsel of information that seemed applicable to future drowning scenarios. And the first thing they'd said was unless you were a trained lifeguard, you should never try to save someone in the water, because they'd likely pull you down in their panic and drown you, too.

But what the heck was she supposed to do? She was in it now. Ugh. She wished she had her whistle. It was just this sort of eventuality that she'd always carried it for. But nat-urally, it was up in her tote bag, in the kitchen. *That darn bag!* thought Kate. *Hillary's right! I need to just ditch it! That stuff is never in the right place at the right time — no sunscreen on the beach, no whistle now! Ugh!*

"Sloan. Give me your hand." Now that Kate was getting mad, it felt better than being scared. As usual, anger temporarily melted her fear away like the sun melting an Awful, Awful on a hot summer afternoon.

But there was no response. "Sloan Bicket!" she commanded in a scary, raw-sounding voice she'd never used before. "Give me your hand this instant or I'm telling everyone that you wet your pants when my ear bled at your house."

The threat worked. There was a pause, and then Kate felt Sloan's limp hand slide into hers, and then grip it hard. A death grip. That's what they'd called it in drown-proofing. But Kate took a deep breath and ordered Sloan, "Now, kick!"

Little by little, Sloan kicked and she pulled, and they made their way to the shallows and then onto the pebbly beach. Sloan crawled up, dragging her right leg behind her, and Kate could barely make her out in the dark. But she could hear Sloan's teeth chattering and wondered if she might be going into shock.

"Sloan. I can't drag you to the Dorm. You have to walk or I have to leave you here."

"No!" cried Sloan in a weak voice.

"Then walk!" barked Kate, feeling more and more like Neeve or Hillary than herself. "You can lean on me."

And they slowly limped their way across the yard, chattering and hobbling together.

Inside the Dorm, the others were changed and in their pj's. Kate and Sloan blinked at the light as they walked inside.

Lark shrieked in horror and then put one hand over her mouth and with the other pointed at Sloan's left shin. Everyone looked down, and there was blood just gushing out of it, and mixing with the water from the sound as it was, it looked like she was about to bleed to death from her leg.

"Oh my God!" Kate nearly swooned again when she looked at Sloan's leg in the light, but this time she stopped herself. Someone had to take care of Sloan, and it wasn't going to be one of the others.

She took a deep breath. "Wait. Okay." She forced herself to be calm and think. "Someone go get towels for us. Someone get a washcloth or . . . maybe another towel for Sloan's leg. Lark, help me get Sloan to the couch. . . ." Oh dear. Their newly slipcovered couch was going to be trashed, but what else could she do?

"Sloan, you're going to be just fine, okay? Everything is alright." Kate felt like she was stepping over her bounds, talking like this to Sloan, but she really felt bad for her. Mrs. Bicket's words were echoing in her head, and Sloan just seemed so pathetic.

Sloan limped to the couch as Neeve dove behind her and settled towels under and around her. Hillary's mouth was set in a grim line, and she quickly squatted in front of Sloan and gathered her leg up into a towel.

"We just need to clear up some blood to see how bad this is," said Hillary.

Sloan was wan and detached, but even through the pity she

felt, Kate did wonder if a part of Sloan was enjoying all the attention. Kate dashed upstairs to change and called down to Phoebe to see if she could borrow something for Sloan to put on, since Phoebe was the only one as tall as she.

Phoebe hesitated, and Kate said, "Oh, for the love of God, Phoebe. The girl is hurt!" And Phoebe snapped out of it and agreed.

Dry and warm, Kate scampered down the ladder from the loft with a hooded hippie warm-up made of hemp or something, and a pair of dark sweatpants.

"Not my Sweetie Sweats!" cried Phoebe, but everyone except Sloan turned and gave her a dirty look, and she shut right up.

"Now," said Kate. "I'm going to get Gee and she can call your mom and see . . ."

"No!" Sloan sat bolt upright out of her trance, and two flaming spots of red appeared in her cheeks. "No! I'll be fine. Just let me stay here for as few more minutes, and then I'll ride home."

"Are you nuts?" demanded Neeve. "She's nuts!" she said, turning to make the announcement to the rest of the group.

Hillary released the towel and winced at the gash. "You definitely need stitches. I think I can even see the bone."

"Oh dear." Kate tried not to look. "Listen, We've got to go get Gee. This is serious! She could even get in trouble for this because it happened at her house. . . ."

Sloan interrupted her again by trying to stand. "I can make

it," she protested, even as her face contracted in a spasm of pain and she collapsed back onto the couch.

"What is the deal with not telling your mom?" asked Kate. She looked at Lark to see if she had any insight into the scenario, since she'd known Sloan the longest and was ostensibly her close friend. But Lark shrugged. They hadn't been hanging out together too much lately, Kate realized. *She's probably become better friends with us in one week than she did with Sloan in one year.*

Sloan looked up at Kate from her stupor and said, "She'll think I'm uncool." Then she dropped her head into her hands.

"What?" asked Kate. She looked around at everyone, and no one said anything, so she pressed on. "What's that supposed to mean?"

"It means I told her I was sleeping here. When Lark bagged me, I said we'd had a change of plans and we were staying at the Callahans'. I didn't want her to know what a loser I was that I'd been bagged."

Everyone was stunned and silent. And then Kate said meekly, "You're worried about your *mom* thinking you're uncool?"

Sloan nodded. "Yes."

The other five exchanged uncomfortable glances, and Sloan still didn't look up. She hadn't been crying until now, but big tears began to drop noiselessly from her eyes onto the towel in her lap.

"What should we do?" mouthed Hillary at Kate.

Heck if I know! thought Kate, and she shrugged. Then she did the thing that always came naturally to her. She went and sat next to Sloan and wrapped her arms around her in a big hug. They sat quietly like that until Sloan's tears seemed to subside, about two minutes — which was an excruciatingly long time for a roomful of people to be silent.

And then Kate said, "Sloan. We need to go tell Gee right now. Neeve is going to go." She nodded at Neeve, and Neeve took off, bolting out the door and up the hill as fast as her skinny little legs could carry her.

"Sloan," Kate continued gently. "Why are you worried that your mom will think you're uncool?"

Sloan didn't lift her head, and her words were kind of muffled by the towel, but maybe that made it easier for her to confess. "Because I have no friends, and I'm a loser."

Kate was shocked. That Sloan Bicket, cool girl, could think of herself as a loser. Why, she might as well have told them she was Martha Stewart herself, here to whip them up a midnight snack! "But you're not a loser, Sloan. You're cool! You're so cool! You're way cooler than me!" Kate said in desperation.

"She is not!" blurted Phoebe.

"Shh!" admonished Hillary, staring daggers at Phoebe.

Kate shot Phoebe a look that said, *Just let me handle this.* She struggled to think of the right thing to say, as the group's unofficial spokesperson. *Things have gone too far*, thought Kate, *when you don't want your own parents to think you're uncool.* She tried to remember Gee's coolness lecture from dinner last week.

"Sloan, coolness is about, ah, style and not substance. It's fleeting. We shouldn't judge people by how they look or what trends they follow. And you really shouldn't be worried whether your parents think you're cool. All parents think their kids are cool, because to them, they are. And, um, we're your friends. Or, I am, anyway." She looked around beseechingly at the others, until they chimed in, too. Of course Phoebe was the last, but at least she piped up.

"You're not a loser, Sloan," Kate added. "I've always thought you were cool."

Sloan sniffed and lifted her head from the towel. "Really?" she asked in a small voice.

"Absolutely." Kate nodded firmly.

Then Gee burst into the room with Neeve and rushed to Sloan's side. She pulled on her reading glasses and grasped Sloan's leg gently in her hand to examine it. She drew in her breath through her teeth in a hiss. "Ouch. You poor dear. Does it hurt like the dickens?"

Kate nearly laughed at Gee's old-fashioned expression, but she was grateful for Gee's compassion as Sloan nodded in mute agony. Kate was grateful that Gee said nothing about the fact that Sloan should've left nearly an hour ago.

"Off we go then, to the clinic. Can you make it up the hill, or should we try to carry you?" Gee asked in concern.

"I can make it. If I have someone to lean on," whispered Sloan.

"I'll go," offered Kate. The others looked like they all might have enjoyed the drama of a trip to the emergency center there, but Gee squashed that idea before it could even take root.

"Neeve, be a love and go tell Sheila where I'm going. Ask if she can keep an ear out for you until I return. Hillary, call Mrs. Bicket. If she's not at home, call the clinic, and if she's not there, just call Ed down at the police station to see if he can track her down for us. Tell her we'll meet her at the emergency room. Now don't worry. Everything is going to be just fine. I'll call Sheila if it seems we need to head off to the mainland for any reason, but I expect not."

The girls nodded at Gee's instructions.

"And no swimming!" she added sternly, as she, Sloan, and Kate headed out the door.

The three struggled up the hill, with Sloan in the middle, protesting halfheartedly that she could do it on her own, and Kate and Gee unwilling to let her try. Gee drove very rapidly but competently to the clinic, and soon they were inside blinking at the fluorescent lights. Everyone there knew Sloan by name, which Kate thought was cool, but seemed to kind of annoy Sloan, as more and more people stopped in to gawk at her and ask where her mother was. Finally, her mother came bursting in in her lab coat, full of apologies and concern. She'd been locked in the lab reviewing X-rays, and her cell phone had been out of range. She'd been unreachable until someone had thought to look for her there.

Sloan really and truly burst into tears when her mother arrived. "Mommy!" she'd wailed, like a little girl, and Kate had had to look away. It was as if Sloan had been keeping it all together until her mother came. The more she saw and learned of the real Sloan underneath the cool girl veneer, the more sympathy Kate felt for her.

Mrs. Bicket was grateful to Gee for bringing Sloan, and Gee was mortified that it had happened at all. She kept apologizing, and Sloan would protest that it was all her fault, she'd been supposed to leave and she hadn't. Then Mrs. Bicket began apologizing, and finally they'd all laughed at the collective "Sorrys" and called it even. And then it was time for Gee and Kate to go home. Sloan would be stitched up right here and would spend the night, just to get an IV drip to make sure she didn't have any infection from the gash.

Kate went to say goodbye to her on the gurney where she was lying, waiting for the surgeon to come. Sloan looked pale, and weak, and unglamorous, and about as unthreatening as possible.

Kate took her hand.

"Sloan, I'm glad you're going to be okay. And don't worry about the stuff you told us. We're all really good at keeping secrets in our family, and we won't betray you. And I'm sorry you weren't sleeping over, too. When you're better, we can set up a sleepover and make it really fun." She smiled encouragingly, and Sloan gave her a faint smile in return, but she gripped Kate's hand hard, harder than Kate would've thought possible, considering her weakened state.

"Thanks," she whispered. "You guys are all so cool."

"You're welcome," said Kate simply.

CHAPTER TWENTY-ONE

Webster's

Of course the cousins and Lark had waited up for Kate, and they wanted all the details of the clinic, and Sloan, and her mom. Kate filled them in, while also protecting Sloan's privacy; she didn't tell them how Sloan had called her mother "Mommy," and cried. It just seemed like an invasion of her privacy and a breaking of trust. It was weird to feel more loyal to Sloan than her cousins, but Kate knew it was the right thing to do. Sloan would be upset if the others thought she was uncool, and even though Kate could see the silliness now of worrying about coolness, she knew Sloan couldn't. She had a way to go.

Gee had gone to say thank you and good night to Sheila, and then came down to the Dorm to check in with the girls and make sure everyone was all right.

"Goodness," she said, perching on the edge of the couch for a brief good-night chat. "Maybe it wasn't such a hot idea to let you all live down here on your own. You seem so far away, and I can't supervise you very well. First it was the car incident, and now this." She bit her lip worriedly, and the girls were quick to defend the Dorm.

Phoebe, in particular, was emphatic. "Gee, don't let one bad apple spoil the whole barrel. Both incidents were instigated by Sloan, and she doesn't even live here."

Gee was thoughtful. "I suppose you're right," she said.

"Sloan does have issues," ventured Lark.

"The poor child. That leg," murmured Gee. And then she turned stern. "There's to be absolutely no swimming after dark. Sloan, and you, Kate, for that matter, could have been even more seriously injured. We're all lucky it wasn't worse."

"Sorry," said Kate. The girls all looked at her with sympathy in their eyes. Everyone knew it hadn't been her fault.

"I know the sequence of events, but how exactly did things spiral out of control down there?" asked Gee.

Kate took a deep breath. "Sloan thought it would be cool to go swimming — that it would make a great story."

"It certainly makes a story, but not a great one," said Gee disapprovingly. "And as for cool, I believe we just had a chat about that the other day, didn't we?"

"Yes." Kate was ashamed.

"I think Sloan is a little mixed up, don't you all?" asked Gee, searching out eye contact with each one of them, even Lark. They all nodded, and she continued. "There's a fine line between bravery and recklessness, boldness and confi-

dence, and it can sometimes be hard to tell the difference."
She paused. "Phoebe, do you have a dictionary down here?"

"Up in the loft. Do you need it now?"

"Yes, please, dear. I just had an idea."

Phoebe scaled the ladder quickly, and the others waited in silence. She returned and handed the dictionary to Gee on her way back to her own seat.

"Ah, *Webster's.*" Gee smiled and hefted the book onto her knees. She lifted the reading glasses that were still hanging around her neck from a chain, and flipped through some pages. "Here we go." She smoothed open the page and began to read.

"Confidence: hmm, hmm, hmm. Umm-hmm. Here we go. 'Faith or belief that one will act in a right, proper, or effective way.' Hmm, hmm. Oh, also, 'A state of mind or a manner marked by easy coolness and freedom from uncertainty, diffidence, or embarrassment.' Now" — she slipped a finger in it to mark her page, and flipped ahead a few pages — "Cool: 'very good, excellent, fashionable.'"

She looked at the girls. "Sloan is certainly confident. But she's brave to the point of, pardon me, but, stupidity and danger. I will grant that she is perhaps cool, as in fashionable. But she is not 'very good or excellent'; she is not someone to emulate or follow. Her confidence makes her seem *right,* when all she is is *sure,* and therein lies the danger of Sloan. Does that make sense?"

The girls nodded, and Gee continued. "I am not here to trash poor Sloan, but I think she is a sad and lonely girl who tries to assert herself by intimidating others because she is not secure enough to simply be herself." She looked around to make sure that everyone understood.

"Confidence is a wonderful thing, but it should be used in conjunction with good sense. Bravery is wonderful as well, but it also needs to encompass an understanding of danger. Kate, what you did tonight, pulling Sloan out of the water, was noble and kind, but it was also reckless and bold, and I wish you hadn't done it. I know you felt that you didn't have a choice, but I would've preferred that you not put yourself in danger to save someone who has done something stupid. If, heaven forbid, there is ever a next time, call for an adult or a trained professional. I'd hate to be taking two girls to the clinic, and one of them my own!"

Kate ducked her head in shame, and Gee reached out to hug her. "You are very brave; I don't mean to imply that you're not. And you've been a very good friend to Sloan, someone who is clearly in need of friendship. So you should be proud of yourself, and relieved that everything turned out fine. But in the future, trust your instincts. If you're scared to do something, then you shouldn't do it."

Kate pulled back to look at Gee. "But what about things like getting donations? I'm scared to do that, but isn't it something I should do?"

"No, not necessarily." Gee shook her head. "If you are truly scared, and you believe it's a reasonable fear, then you shouldn't do it. But if you know deep down inside that you're being unreasonable, and you're actually just nervous or could get through the job with someone to help you, then you need to figure out a strategy for accomplishing the things that are only nerve-racking and not dangerous."

Kate sat in silence, mulling this over. The others looked at her with wide eyes, and a newfound respect in them that was almost like intimidation. They weren't used to her doing dangerous things.

Gee looked at Kate. "Are you alright, dear?"

Kate smiled suddenly. "Yes. Just thinking."

"It's awfully late and it's been quite a night. You really do need to head off to sleep now, girls. And no more monkey business." She frowned an exaggerated frown. "Come along. Up to bed with you." Lark was sleeping on an air mattress in the loft with them, so they all rose to say good night to Gee and climb the ladder.

Up in bed, snuggled safely under her covers, Kate thought about everything Gee had said. She knew now that she'd been mistaking confidence for coolness, as far as Sloan was concerned, but she also knew she needed to work on her own confidence. It would serve her well to be more confident in general.

"Ahhh," Kate sighed aloud. It was hard figuring stuff out. Maybe this was what growing up was all about.

"Kate?" It was Phoebe.

"Umm-hmm?"

"I'm sorry I've been so grumpy about Sloan."

Kate sat up. "It's okay. I know you were just trying to protect me."

"There's something else, too. I'm scared to do a lot of things, too, like you, and I felt like if I commiserated with you and let my paranoia get the better of me, then I'd never get out there and do anything brave or fun."

Kate thought for a moment about how Phoebe had been somewhat of a scaredy-cat when the summer had started, too. But then she'd come around because, as she said, she had all kinds of adventures when she was with the cousins that she might not normally have on her own. It was true for Kate, too.

"I'm sorry if I was holding you back," offered Kate.

"No. You weren't. I just wasn't being kind because I was worried about myself."

"It's okay." Kate paused. "You know, Phoebe, Sloan's not all bad, by the way."

Lark spoke up now, and Kate was mildly embarrassed that she'd been listening. "Yeah, when she lets her guard down and stops trying to be cool, she can actually be really nice."

"Shhh!" said Neeve. "Group therapy time is over. I'm tired."

Kate giggled. "Okay, sleepyhead." And she laid her head back down on her pillow. Even though what she had done tonight was stupid, she was a tiny bit proud of herself for doing it. It was so unlike her. It was such a cool, no, *confident* thing to have done. And it would make a great story, as Sloan had predicted. Just not for a while.

"Guys?" whispered Kate. "Cousins forever!"

"Cousins forever!" they whispered back.

Chapter Twenty-Two

Being a Friend

Saturday dawned a gorgeous blue, with a lemony sun that washed over everything and brightened it, making each leaf on each tree look crisp and clear. It was perfect weather for the benefit, and Gee was clearly relieved. Five hundred guests in a backyard muddied by rain would've been unbearable.

The girls hung around the house, watching the final stages of preparation, and helping out whenever Gee needed it. They watched Nate Spangleman's team arrange fluffy blue hydrangeas into billowy groups and then insert them into glass bowls bedecked with ribbons. Then they watched the caterers unload the food and start cooking. Kate hung around, trying to sneak a peek at their mobile operations in the small tent they'd set up off Gee's kitchen. Gee had told her they were doing a mostly organic menu, with all heart-healthy, cancer-preventing foods, since it was for a health clinic, and Kate was thrilled. She planned on getting some recipes from them for her new journal later.

▲

Soon enough, it was time to dress for the party. Kate had a beautiful pink dress to wear, and she fluffed her hair up into pretty curls with some gel and barretted one of Gee's "Old Blush" roses into it, above her right ear. Phoebe produced a pair of clip-on earrings that looked like pierced, and it didn't even hurt Kate's injured ear to wear them. She felt beautiful and, for lack of a better word, secure. She wasn't tan (but at least she wasn't orange); her hair and her eyebrows looked great; her ears weren't pierced, but they looked it; she wasn't "in shape," but at least she knew what her body was capable of (such as saving people from drowning), and she knew she was on the road to being healthier; she didn't have new interests but instead had come to appreciate her old ones. And she was certainly braver. She felt happier than she had in a long time, happy to be herself.

▲

The benefit was a smashing success. The backyard was crowded, and delicious food was passed around by Coolidge's. The night darkened, and all of the candles on the tables glittered and illuminated the smiling faces of the guests, decked out in their beautiful dressy outfits, so unlike their everyday wear. Miss Munsfield was there, and Nate Spangleman —

dressed outlandishly in a cape and a ruffly pirate shirt — and Mr. Bradshaw, and the lady from the fabric store; Farren from the Little Store; and the Bickets. The auction brought in nearly fifty thousand dollars, as people good-naturedly bid up inexpensive items so as to raise money for the clinic. It was fun to watch, and Kate got a particular kick out of watching Neeve bid for the Gullboutique pashminas for Gee.

Neeve had suggested to the others that they buy them for Gee as a thank-you present for having them all summer, and everyone had agreed. They'd pooled their funds and set a limit of $400 for the present, gasping at the amount, but willing to pay it because, truth be told, it was their parents' money, anyway. They'd spent hardly any of it since they'd arrived because Gee was always picking up the tab. So when the item had come along in the auction, Neeve had raised a paddle she borrowed from Farren, and set her jaw, determined to secure the gift and preparing for a long fight against other bidders.

But the crowd quickly realized that it was a "child" who was bidding, and the other bidders dropped out so that Neeve would win. She was triumphant when she secured the lot for $150, and the cousins shrieked and jumped in the air, clapping her on the back.

Kate had another moment of pleasure when she'd watched the bidding for a "Kate Callahan Original" sweater. Some strangers bid for it, perhaps in tribute to Gee, but it was Mrs. Bicket who bid the longest and eventually won it for $1,500! Kate was shocked that anyone would pay so much for a sweater, especially by a kid like her — even though she was a decent knitter. But she was even more shocked when Mrs. Bicket came up to her later in the night and announced her happiness at having won it. "Sloan told me not to even bother coming home if I didn't get it for her!" she'd said, and Kate had grinned.

"I would've made her one for free!" she replied, and Mrs. Bicket had demurred, saying she was happy to pay the money for such a good cause.

The girls roamed the crowd selling raffle tickets at cocktail time, and then they started up once more after dinner had been served. They each had a wicker basket with pale blue ribbons tied decoratively to the handle, and the ribbons fluttered out in a pretty way as the girls walked. Much to Kate's surprise, selling raffle tickets wasn't hard for her at all. Maybe it was because she was secure in her surroundings, being that the party was basically at her home. Or maybe it was all she'd learned that week, about herself and others. Perhaps it was the final donation she'd gotten from Farren that tipped the scales in favor of confidence. But it mostly had something to do with the fact that she wasn't asking for "something for nothing." She asked people to buy a ticket, they gave her money, and she gave them a ticket. So it wasn't like trick-or-treating, or soliciting donations. Instead it was a transaction; it was sales. And Kate was excellent at it. She'd describe the wonderful array of prizes so eloquently, imparting so many sensual details and loving descriptions of the items that people couldn't give her their money fast enough. She'd take it from them, still with a dreamy expression in her eye, and she'd laugh as she promised she'd get their name picked at raffle time. Much to her surprise, she sold out of tickets before anyone else — even Sloan, who had sort of a sympathy thing going, what with the huge bandage on her leg.

At the end of the night, the crowd hushed, and raffle tickets were drawn. Kate was stunned to hear her name called out not once, but twice. First, she won the mini-golf outing for eight people. She walked to the bandstand in a daze to collect her coupon, and when she returned to her seat, she didn't even remember making the trip. But the second time, as the prize was announced, she was holding her breath to see who the winner was. It was a free ear piercing at Gullboutique. Distractedly she wondered who had gotten that donation, since it hadn't been on the master list, nor had Sloan bragged about it that day when she'd gotten the pashmina donation. Huh. But as she puzzled about the origins of it, she was again electrified by the sound of her name over the tinny PA system. Her cousins hooted and hollered, and she even saw Sloan clapping wildly for her from across the tent. Gee was handing out the coupons for the emcee, and she gave Kate a hug as she came to claim it.

"We'll just have to talk your parents into it," she whispered in Kate's ear.

"Thanks, Gee," Kate replied.

Strangely, when she returned to her seat and opened the

coupon envelope, the gift wasn't written out on Gullboutique letterhead, as Sloan's donation had been. And the handwriting on the sheet of stationery looked strangely familiar.

Gee!

Kate's jaw dropped, and she searched out Gee's eyes again up on stage. Gee felt her gaze and turned, and when their eyes met, Gee winked. Ha! Kate clapped her hands gleefully and now she had no doubt that she'd be getting her ears pierced as soon as possible. Gee wouldn't have staged this if she had any reason to believe that Kate's parents would say no.

When it was all over, Kate already knew that she had just had one of the best days of her life. The cousins — along with Lark — were sitting around a cleared table with their shoes kicked off in the grass and sodas on the table before them. The party rental people had arrived and were breaking down all the tables and chairs, and the kitchen staff from Coolidge's were rounding up miscellaneous glassware under the now brightly lit tent. Gee was at another table having a relaxing cup of decaf with the other people from the committee, making notes for next year's benefit while the details were still fresh in their minds. Sloan had left with her parents, her mother forgoing the committee meeting in order to stay with Sloan. Kate was happy, thinking of how happy Sloan had looked to be leaving with both of them. Lark's voice interrupted her musings.

"Kate. That is so awesome about your ear piercing! Your grandmother is so cool!" said Lark. Kate winced at the adjective; she was tired of coolness. "And to think that your parents had said you had to be thirteen, and now they're obviously going to let you do it sooner. Wow!" But whereas just a few days ago she would've been put off by Lark's enthusiasm and her memory for the details of Kate's parents' rules, tonight she felt warmly toward Lark for caring.

"Thanks," she said with a happy smile. "This had been the best day ever!"

Later that night, as she lay in bed thinking back on the party, and all the stress of the two weeks preceding it, Kate decided that the bravest thing she'd ever done — yes, the coolest thing — was to become Sloan's friend.

She sat up in her bed and grabbed her To Do book out of the drawer in her bedside table. The outdoor lights illuminated the room just enough so that she could see what she was doing. She turned to her New Me list and uncapped her pen, then she drew a huge X through the list.

Next, she turned the page, smoothing it out thoughtfully, and began a new list.

THINGS I'M GOOD AT
Knitting
Baking
Singing

Painting
Flowers
Decorating

She paused and wrote,

Being a friend.

Then she closed the book, tucked it and the pen away, and lay back down, feeling secure and happy.

"Cousins forever!" she whispered into the darkness.

"Cousins forever!" Lark whispered back.

And Kate smiled.

Meet
The Callahan Cousins

Do you have a favorite Callahan cousin?
Are you dying to know more about her?
Here are some vital tidbits about each of
the girls . . . some of which you might
not already know!

Hillary Miranda Callahan
Hometown: Boulder, Colorado

Hillary's Favorites: Downhill skiing, running, exploring, science, Merrell clogs, Sweetie Sweats, shrimp fajitas, and her golden retriever Winnie (named after Winnie the Pooh when Hillary was five).

Biggest fear: Being cut out of the Callahan cousin loop if her parents get divorced.

Find out more about Hillary in *The Callahan Cousins: Summer Begins* as Hillary leads the cousins in a quest to defend the Callahan family's honor when the girls find themselves caught up in an old rivalry involving a lost island, ancient family lore, and eccentric islanders. Will Hillary prove herself as the Callahan family hero, or will she get herself sent home?

NEEVE ORLA CALLAHAN

Hometown: Good question! Born in Galway, Ireland, and has lived in Kenya, China, and now lives in Singapore.

Neeve's Favorites: Clothes with an ethnic twist, traveling, meeting new people, black coffee, Japanese techno music, soccer, languages (she speaks Swahili, Chinese, and French).

Biggest secret: Neeve loves traveling and living in eccentric places, but she has always secretly longed for a real place to call home. Neeve has decided this summer is the perfect opportunity to make Gull Island her home.

Find out more about Neeve in *The Callahan Cousins: Home Sweet Home.* Grandmother Gee has given the cousins permission to fix up and move into the Dorm—their very own quarters separate from the main house! But in the midst of their redecorating mania, Neeve stumbles upon a troubling family secret that she's reluctant to share even with her cousins.

Kate

MARY KATHERINE CALLAHAN
Hometown: New York City

Kate's Favorites: Cooking, needlepoint, painting, decorating, beef Wellington, preppy clothes, her gold charm bracelet, anything by Beatrix Potter, and generally feeling cozy.

Why she loves her cousins: They bring out the best in her. Kate tends to complicate things by being such a perfectionist, and she lets her fears hold her back from new experiences. Spending the summer with her cousins has shown her it's okay to be herself, but it's also okay not to be perfect.

Find out more about Kate in *The Callahan Cousins: Keeping Cool*. When the usually shy Kate launches a quest to become the "cool" girl in town, her over-the-top antics threaten to pull the cousins apart. Will the new Kate rule the day, or will the cousins save her before it's too late?

Phoebe

PHOEBE ANNE CALLAHAN
Hometown: Winter Park, Florida

Phoebe's Favorites: Reading (books, newspapers, magazines, etc.), hippie clothes, Swedish meatballs, Diet Coke, tennis, her leather-bound dictionary, and Uni-ball pens (because they make her handwriting look really good).

What she doesn't want her cousins to know: She worships her big sister, Daphne.

Find out more about Phoebe in *The Callahan Cousins: Book Four* coming in October 2006. When the girls spend the night in the whaling museum, Phoebe must come to terms with her fears and the fact that she may not know everything.

Liz Carey is a former children's book editor. She lives in New York City with her husband and two young sons, and she has twenty-five first cousins of her own.